TAWNY ROSE

Katherine Kent

TAWNY ROSE

Katherine Kent

**A Judy Sullivan Book
Walker and Company
New York**

First published in the United States of America
in 1984 by the Walker Publishing Company, Inc.

Published simultaneously in Canada by John Wiley & Sons
Canada, Limited, Rexdale, Ontario.

Library of Congress Cataloging in Publication Data

Kent, Katherine, 1937—
    Tawny rose.

    "A Judy Sullivan book."
    I. Title.
PS3561.E519T3   1984   813'.54   83-40426
ISBN 0-8027-0775-0

Printed in the United States of America

10   9   8   7   6   5   4   3   2   1

Chapter One

THE WINTER GALE shrieked along the Cornish coast, lashing every cove and inlet, trying to pluck fishing boats from their moorings. As the London coach precariously made its way to the courtyard of the Inn of the Blue Lantern, the smugglers within frantically tried to conceal their contraband. It was 1789, and they had much to fear if their passage from war-ravaged France with wine and spirits was discovered.

Darcy Sinclair, however, was unaware of the furor her arrival on the coach was causing. After all, so much had happened in the past week that the local innkeeper and his patrons acting strangely seemed of little consequence.

She stepped into the welcoming warmth of the inn's public room and quickly removed her hooded cloak. Hair not quite red, nor yet golden, but equal parts of both, emphasized by tawny shadows, fought to be free of restraining pins. Large cinnamon-colored eyes traveled around the room and came to rest on the man leaning nonchalantly against the bar, the man who was regarding her with insolent admiration.

As she turned to face him, the blue light of the inn's lantern fully illuminated her face. The man straightened up as though hit by lightning. His striking features registered shock as he stepped forward with an unintelligible exclamation on his lips. He had the attitude of a man seeing a ghost.

His obvious astonishment was disturbing, for Darcy had

never seen the man before and knew that if they had ever met she would have remembered him. As they watched each other intently for a moment, Darcy was vaguely aware that several men were hastily carrying barrels and kegs through a door to the rear of the inn.

"You, sir," Darcy said. "Are you the innkeeper? I require a room for the night." She spoke more imperiously than she had intended, feeling uncomfortable under the man's intense scrutiny.

He bowed with casual grace. In the flickering blue light of the oil lamp Darcy saw that he had the dark good looks of a Cornishman. Black hair, swarthy skin. Mobile black eyebrows raised expressively over eyes the deep blue of a twilit sea. This man, however, was much taller than most Cornishmen, and Darcy realized as he moved closer that his shirt was of fine linen and his chamois breeches and Hessian boots of better quality than those of the other men present.

"I would be most happy to share *my* room with mam'selle," he said. Although he used the French term, there was no trace of a French accent, yet not the Cornish accent Darcy expected to hear.

"Begging your pardon, miss." A portly man stepped forward. He was red in the face from the exertion of having heaved a keg into the back room. "I be the innkeeper, milady. We weren't expecting the coach to stop 'ere tonight, but I'll find ye a room." He threw a stern glance in the direction of the well-dressed man. "Captain Winslow was just joking, milady."

"Stede Winslow. At your service, mam'selle." Before Darcy realized what he was about to do, he had captured her hand in steel-strong fingers and had raised it to his lips. She felt the hot imprint of his mouth on her wrist and tried to suppress a shiver either from apprehension or excitement. Everything about Stede Winslow seemed to exude danger, from the undisguised appraisal in his eyes to the careless intimacy of his touch.

"Hadn't the captain best be making hisself scarce?" the innkeeper asked pointedly, with a jerk of his head in the direction of the rear room.

Darcy was as surprised by the innkeeper's insolence toward a patron as she was by Captain Winslow's lack of propriety in approaching a strange young woman so boldly.

Winslow said, "Our transaction is far from complete, landlord. But it can await my lady's pleasure." He turned to Darcy. "Before you retire perhaps you would like a hot toddy to ward off the chill of the night?"

Darcy glanced about the public bar. There were no female patrons. A buxom barmaid was polishing glasses behind the bar and giving both Captain Winslow and Darcy frosty glances.

Since Winslow's invitation was insultingly ill-bred, Darcy turned to the innkeeper and said, "Would you be so kind as to show me to my room? I'm expecting someone to come here for me in the morning. *Sir Laurence Tregarth.*" She pronounced the name as though it were a weapon to ward off the dark innuendo of Captain Winslow's glance.

Winslow bowed again and gestured with his hand for her to proceed after the innkeeper, who started toward the staircase. "Far be it from me to detain Sir Laurence's lady," Winslow said, a mocking glint replacing the former admiration in his eyes.

Ridiculously, Darcy wanted to say that she was not Sir Laurence's lady—nor anyone else's for that matter—and that if it were the prerogative of a young lady to choose a suitor, it would be her beloved Cullen.

Darcy had barely reached the staircase when she heard the sound of horses' hooves clattering into the courtyard. A frantic shout, louder than the rising wind, froze everyone where they stood.

"Excise men! Hard on my heels!" the rider yelled as he burst through the door.

Instantly all was confusion. Some of the men jammed the narrow doorway leading to the rear room while others drew the long wooden bolt on the front door and peered through the diamond-paned windows into the darkness beyond. The barmaid ducked down behind the bar.

A shot rang out, and a pistol ball thudded into the stout wooden door. Someone slammed the shutters closed on the windows.

"Open! In the name of His Majesty!" came the hail from outside.

Most of the men attempting to get through the rear door had now disappeared from view, except one who paused and called to Captain Stede Winslow. "Come on, cap'n, or you'll be swinging from a different kind of rigging."

Stede Winslow grinned, bowed deeply in Darcy's direction, and said, "First I must escort the lady to safety." There were sounds of a battering ram hitting the inn door.

"Quick milady—up the stairs," the innkeeper urged.

A second shot rang out, and Darcy found herself propelled up the stairs by Captain Stede Winslow. When they came to her room, he opened the door for her, and, with a sweeping bow, was gone. Darcy slipped the bolt of the lock, then placed a chair in front of the door. Sounds of shouting and crashes from below continued for several minutes.

She sat on the bed and wondered if the entire inn would tumble about her ears. Her London friends had warned her about Cornwall. It was an untamed place peopled by ferocious men who *boasted* of their lack of English blood, but nothing had prepared her for a welcome such as this.

Darcy shivered, realizing that her clothing was damp. The last she remembered, the coachman had been unloading her trunk as she raced for shelter from the icy wind and driving rain.

For a moment her brittle composure threatened to crack. She had undoubtedly traveled to a land where the people were as wild and dangerous as the rugged coastline she had seen on her long journey.

The sounds below gradually diminished and were followed

by a silence that seemed even more threatening. Peering through the tiny casement window, Darcy could see nothing but rain splattering against the black glass. Her teeth were chattering. She began to peel away her skirt and petticoats. Unfastening the hooks of her blouse with numb fingers, Darcy allowed herself the luxury of a single tear. She brushed her knuckles across her brow, blinking in the strangeness of the austere room. Its sole furnishings were a marble-topped washstand, a four-poster bed with a patchwork quilt, and the chair in front of the door, her last line of defense. A tiled fireplace contained the dreary remains of a long-dead fire. On the mantlepiece, a lantern glowed fretfully, emitting eerie blue light like all of the inn's lanterns. No doubt the result of tinting the glass.

The room was a bleak contrast to the one she had shared with three other girls at the Grafton School for Young Ladies. Darcy thought of that last night at school, and the bewilderment at the shattering of her world came flooding back.

The girls had been engaged in one of their favorite after-lights-out discussions. *What exactly did a husband do to a wife in the marriage bed?* After all, Leticia had giggled, within a few months they would all leave the Grafton School forever and plunge into the whirl of "coming out" balls and parties. Each of them would undoubtedly be married before a year had passed. They really needed more explicit information.

"Darcy promised to ask Cullen," Ann said reproachfully.

"I think she *did* ask him and simply won't tell us," Leticia put in.

"Or perhaps," Mary put in with a shiver of delicious horror, "It is simply too awful to contemplate, and Darcy is sparing us the terrible details."

Darcy had laughed and pondered over the fact that every one of their conversations managed to circle back to Cullen. The girls were, of course, madly in love with him despite the fact that they had met him only when he visited Darcy on special holidays. Unlike the other pupils, Darcy lived all year at the Grafton School because she had no relatives in England.

"Do tell!" Leticia begged. "None of us has a rake for a brother to ask."

"Cullen is *not* my brother," Darcy explained for the hundredth time. "He is the son of my stepfather. Shortly before my mother died, she married a widower with a son. And you mustn't believe what Cullen said about being a rake. He was teasing you. He graduated from university recently and will no doubt be joining his father abroad."

"Well, he's your adopted brother, then," Ann said. "And it surely must be illegal for you to marry him."

"You're just too much competition for the rest of us," Mary sighed.

Their whispers came to an abrupt end as their door was suddenly and unexpectedly opened. Miss Blenning, the headmistress, stood on the threshold, a candle in a pewter holder illuminating thin grey plaits hanging over her dressing gown and pince-nez slightly askew on her aquiline nose as she peered into the now silent room. The four girls were rigid beneath satin quilts as Miss Blenning made her way cautiously to the nearest bed. She looked down at Leticia, then moved on to the next bed, and, recognizing Darcy, patted her cheek.

"Wake up, Darcy. You must come downstairs immediately."

Darcy stumbled out of bed, found her dressing gown and slippers, and followed Miss Blenning down the stairs and into the visitors' sitting room. Blinking, Darcy saw a caped figure standing in front of the fireplace. The next moment she was flinging herself into Cullen's arms.

"Forgive the dramatics," Cullen said, his dark eyes flashing briefly at the hovering figure of Miss Blenning, "But I must be on a ship crossing the Channel at dawn."

"Goodness! You're not going to France in these perilous times!" Darcy exclaimed. "But why—"

"No time to explain now. Father has returned to England— to Cornwall to be more precise. He wants you to go to him immediately. He has acquired a large house and needs you to run it for him. Darcy, we know you will be disappointed at missing all of the parties and celebrations in London that girls leaving school normally have . . . but Father promises that you will have a grand coming-out ball in Cornwall later on. I shall be going there myself within a few weeks."

Darcy's heart leapt at this announcement. "Of course I shall go at once," she said. "Sir Laurence has provided for me all these years, and I shall be only too happy to repay his generosity in any way I can." At that moment she gazed adoringly into Cullen's black eyes and suppressed the unreasonable fear that tugged at her heart when she remembered the bleak and terrifying—but mercifully infrequent—visits of her stepfather, Sir Laurence Tregarth.

Cullen gave her instructions to go to the Inn of the Blue Lantern and wait there, Tregarth Hall being some distance from the coach stops. The following morning, Darcy bade her friends a tearful good-bye, and Miss Blenning put her on the first of the coaches that would take her to Cornwall.

In her room at the Inn of the Blue Lantern, Darcy slipped under the quilt on the hard bed, wearing only her damp chemise and pantelettes. She was shaking from the cold and hoped someone would shortly bring up her luggage so that she might change into a warm nightgown.

Her room was panelled with dark wood, and on either side of the tiled fireplace were shelves evidently intended for books but devoid of anything but a film of dust. Darcy's eyes were becoming heavy with fatigue and her numbed bones gradually relaxed under the scratchy warmth of the quilt. She was sure she had fallen asleep and was dreaming when the shelves on one side of the fireplace slowly resolved and the silhouette emerged from the darkness beyond.

She sat bolt upright in bed, clutching the quilt to her breast.

The lantern on the mantelpiece cast its blue light on Captain Stede Winslow. A raffish grin appeared on his face, thrown into relief in the ghostly light, and she felt a thrill of pure horror move icily down her spine. Before she had time to open her mouth to scream, he had leapt across the room and was beside her on the narrow bed, his hand closing firmly over her mouth.

"Promise not to scream," he demanded. His mouth was close to her ear and his breath warm against her throat. "After all, it's your fault I could not make good my escape with my men. If I had not tarried to admire the loveliest creature I have ever seen, I should be halfway back to France by now."

His grip relaxed slightly, and Darcy promptly sank her teeth into his hand, then drew a deep breath ready to emit a scream guaranteed to wake the dead. He was too quick for her, however, and this time it was not his hand that went to her mouth but his lips in a fierce and hungry kiss.

For a second she thought she must swoon as his warm lips and darting tongue explored her mouth with practiced barbarism. Something was pounding painfully against her ribs and she realized dimly that it was her own heart, thumping madly as Stede Winslow pushed her backward, imprisoning her body with the lean hardness of his own. The kiss had begun too unexpectedly to resist, but now she struggled and tried to turn her head from that devouring mouth.

He raised his head and looked down at her, deep blue eyes piercing through her fright and anger to the inexplicable feeling of warmth that had come welling up from deep inside her. While she panted, trying to regain her breath and collect her wits, he said softly, "If you call for help, I shall tell them you hid me here. And then, lovely lady with the beguiling eyes, what will Sir Laurence say?"

"What do you want of me?" She gasped out the words and tried not to imagine what his answer would be in view of the pressure of his body and the certain knowledge that he was very much enjoying their closeness. A little devil in the back of her mind was whispering that in one brief moment the answer to all the girls' questions about the marriage bed might be revealed to her.

Stede Winslow chuckled, "Why," he said, "to spend the night with you, of course."

Chapter Two

STEDE WINSLOW'S CONVERSATION would perhaps have made more sense to her had she not been pressed between the unyielding surface of the bed and his muscular body. Completely unconcerned, he spoke amiably, almost apologetically.

"In a few minutes the dull-witted Excise men will begin a search of the inn," he was saying, while all the time she was acutely aware of his thigh rubbing against her own. "If you will be so kind as to call out that you are awaiting the arrival of Sir Laurence Tregarth and that you are quite alone, I am sure that they will go away and we will not be troubled further."

Darcy hoped that the blue light cast by the lantern on the mantlepiece was concealing the hot stain she knew infused her cheeks. "And what if I call to them instead that the fugitive they are seeking is holding me prisoner?" she inquired breathlessly.

"Surely you wouldn't turn me over to the Excise officers after all we've been to each other?"

Darcy let out her breath cautiously, afraid that any sudden movement on her part might bring disaster. She was, after all, wearing only a fine lawn chemise and pantellettes, both in an unseemly state of disarray. "Will you promise to leave immediately if I agree to help you escape the Excise men?"

She was gathering her wits about her, and it had occurred to her that—for the time being—it would be prudent to humor him. There was really no alternative, since she certainly wasn't strong enough to fight off his advances.

Stede Winslow raised up on his elbows and looked down at her. She knew her breast was bare, but her arms were trapped at her sides. "Are you related in some way to Sir Laurence?"

"Yes."

"But you have never lived with Tregarth. No one at the inn knew who you were."

"Will you please get up? I'm beginning to get a knot in my neck. I give you my word I'll not tell the Excise men you are hiding in my room if you in turn will promise not to . . . not to. . . ."

"Rape you?" he asked, a small smile hovering about the corners of his mouth.

Mercifully, she did not have to comment on this as the sound of heavy footsteps on the stairs and then the pounding on guest-room doors signalled that the search had begun.

Darcy tried to speak calmly when a voice in the hall called out, "Open the door if you please. We are looking for an armed and dangerous criminal. Open, in the name of the King!"

"There's no one but me in here, and I'm waiting for my trunk to be sent up. I'm Miss Sinclair, waiting here for Sir Laurence Tregarth. You will be answerable to him if you dare invade my room. Please inquire of the innkeeper as to the whereabouts of my luggage."

Stede Winslow grinned at her, then rolled off the bed and sprang as lightly as a cat to the door. He stood waiting, poised to tackle anyone who tried to enter. Darcy saw now that he was not armed.

The disembodied voice called, "Sorry to have bothered you, milady." The footsteps moved on.

Outside, the wind howled in the eaves, and the rain roared against the windowpanes.

Stede Winslow moved back toward the bed, and Darcy clutched the quilt to her as she inched away from him. "I can call him back," she whispered fiercely.

"No need, Miss Sinclair. At least you don't bear the hated

name of Tregarth." Although he pronounced the name Tregarth with considerable distaste, his look revealed that he was mesmerized by the ripe body and lovely face, haughty with proper outrage, yet illuminated by eyes as saucy as any doxie's. "Because," he continued, his teeth flashing white against his swarthy skin as he smiled broadly, "I suspect we have only just begun a very interesting relationship, you and I."

He pressed some unseen mechanism that caused the bookshelves to revolve. "A passage through the wall links this room to the next. Shall I show you how to operate it in case you wish to join me to finish what we so tantalizingly started?"

"If you haven't disappeared by the time I count to three," Darcy said through gritted teeth. "One. Two. . . . ."

Stede Winslow bowed, and grinning, stepped through the apperture.

Darcy jumped from the bed and began to pull on her clothes with shaking fingers. As soon as she was decently dressed, she removed the chair from before her door and went quickly down to the public room.

The Excise men were hauling barrels and kegs from the back room. The innkeeper, his face so red it seemed he must shortly succumb to apoplexy, stood with his hands in the air. He was guarded by a man with a pistol, who in turn stared admiringly at the buxom barmaid.

Darcy cleared her throat and said, "Innkeeper . . . I really need my luggage. My clothes are drenched."

The man who appeared to be in charge said, "Go and bring the lady's trunk, innkeeper."

When the innkeeper returned, Darcy fixed accusing eyes on him, and, bending over her trunk so the others would not hear, said, "And you will provide me with a different room. One without bookshelves if you please."

She awoke to clear skies and pale winter sunshine. Her window overlooked the sea, and she saw that the inn was built on a sheer cliff over a rocky cove. On the other side of the inlet was a cluster of cottages and fish cellars, jumbled together precariously close to the water.

The sea churned restlessly in the cove, breaking white and fierce over the dark rocks and surging into hidden caves and inlets. So many places for boats and small ships to hide, Darcy thought. It was no wonder the smugglers brought their French wines and spirits to the Inn of the Blue Lantern.

In the comforting brightness of the morning, her encounter with Captain Stede Winslow had taken on all the qualities of an adventurous dream. His hungry kiss and impertinent caress, to say nothing of the Customs and Excise officers pursuing him, would have made a breathtaking yarn to spin for the girls of the Grafton School.

Darcy told herself sternly that well-brought-up young ladies did not seek such adventures and certainly should not boast of them. She dressed and went downstairs.

The splintered front door was the only sign that there had been a running battle between smugglers and Excise men the night before. When Darcy inquired of the innkeeper what the outcome had been, he shrugged and winked at her.

"They didn't catch any of them, milady. Oh, they confiscated the spirits, but they couldn't do nothing to me, see, 'cause I was at the mercy of the fair traders meself." He placed a plate of crisply fried fish in front of her and was about to give her another elaborate wink when he remembered who he was confiding in. His face grew beet red. "Not that I have any dealings with fair traders willingly. You will assure Sir Laurence that I don't, won't you milady? And I do apologize to you again for forgetting that Cap'n Winslow knew about the connecting panel to the room you was in."

Darcy picked up her steaming mug of tea and took a scalding sip. "Who is he? Does he live in these parts? He doesn't sound like a Cornishman . . . nor an Englishman or Frenchman for that matter."

The barmaid came into the room carrying a tray of aromatic fresh bread. She giggled, biting her lip, as the innkeeper wiped his hands nervously on his apron. "No . . . no, that he doesn't. I really don't know him at all. He has a schooner that puts in here from time to time. He first started coming about the time Sir Laurence arrived. If you'll excuse us, Violet and me must finish cleaning up the mess the Excise men made in back. Put that bread down, Violet, and get on with it." He glared at the barmaid.

"All right, Dad. No need to shout," Violet responded tartly. She tossed a ringlet of bright red hair back over her plump shoulder and flounced out of the room.

"Albert is my name, milady. Ring the bell if you want more tea or anything," the innkeeper said.

Darcy had barely finished breakfast when Sir Laurence's carriage arrived to take her to Tregarth Hall.

The steep and winding road led through breathtakingly beautiful countryside, but Darcy was more aware of the vast and awesome presence of the sea. It breathed and sighed like a great living being, clutching at the land as though seeking a union that was forever doomed. Like an impossible love, Darcy thought.

Tregarth Hall loomed ahead, stark and ominous against the pale sky. Darcy's first thought was that it should still be called by its original name, Channel Castle. It had been built as a fortress in 1450 to withstand the assaults of French coastal raiders. As her carriage approached, Darcy could see two portcullis entrances with machicolations above that were a grim reminder of the fact that at one time, unwelcome visitors had been greeted by showers of molten lead and other missiles. There were five towers with gun embrasures and a high crenellated curtain wall.

Cullen had told her a little about her new home before she left London. She knew that the narrow peninsula from the mainland to the point upon which the castle was built had eroded with the passing centuries. Tregarth Hall now stood on a desolate bluff, separated from the mainland by the sea and accessible by a stout bridge built over churning white water and jagged rocks.

Once inside, Darcy saw that most of the renovations Cullen had mentioned were interior ones. She stepped into a central hall encircled by graceful pillars reaching to an upper gallery that appeared to be of recent vintage. She hoped Sir Laurence Tregarth's somewhat forbidding exterior concealed a warmer core.

Darcy had met Sir Laurence briefly prior to her mother's marriage to him. She had been dismayed that her lovely and vivacious mother had chosen to spend the rest of her life with a man of brooding countenance and apparent lack of humor. Sir Laurence was rich, of course, and Darcy supposed some would find his hooded eyes and somewhat dissipated handsomeness appealing. There had been many times when Darcy fervently hoped that Cullen would not become as frighteningly arrogant as his father in later life, for there was an unmistakable physical resemblance between the two.

She had never known whether Sir Laurence had made her mother happy during their brief marriage. They had departed for the distant Indies, and the first communication she had received was a letter from Sir Laurence advising her to expect his son, Cullen, to visit her at school shortly. Cullen had brought the news that her mother had died of yellow fever almost the moment she arrived in the Caribbean.

As the servants fussed around her in the hall, Darcy heard Sir Laurence's voice angrily berating a groom who had apparently neglected a favorite mare. A moment later Sir Laurence came striding across the hall, polished leather riding boots eating up the distance. He carried a riding crop, which he tossed impatiently from one hand to the other.

"Darcy, my dear. Welcome to Tregarth Hall," he said, bending to kiss her cheek. His lips were cool. Eyes that were Cullen's eyes—though cynical instead of teasing—searched her expression and demeanor. "Come, we'll go into the library while the servants take your trunk up to your room. Have you no other luggage?" He spoke briskly, and the servants leapt to obey commands he had not yet given.

Following him into the library, where a log roared in the fireplace, Darcy felt a twinge of dread. She was aware for the first time that she had left forever the safety of the all-female world of the Grafton School for Young Ladies. The world of flint-eyed men with its undercurrent of danger and intrigue into which she had been so unceremoniously thrust had found her unprepared. She squared her shoulders slightly as Sir Laurence spoke briefly of her mother.

"You will find a jewel box in your room that belonged to her. I deemed it advisable to save the contents for you until now." The hooded eyes studied Darcy for a moment, then Sir Laurence continued, "She wanted you to be educated in England just as I wanted Cullen to be. I trust you understand that my business kept me abroad and that you do not feel I neglected you all these years. Despite my apparent lack of interest, I can assure you that Cullen has kept me informed of your welfare and progress."

"You were most generous to me, Sir Laurence," Darcy replied. "I fear I would have been in dire straits without your financial aid." Her eyes lit up, glowing tawny gold. "Cullen has always been more than a brother to me."

Sir Laurence frowned suddenly and turned to gaze into the roaring flames in the fireplace.

Unaware that she had given her guardian a glimpse of her infatuation for his son, Darcy waited as the silence between them lengthened.

"Cullen has not been toying with your affections, I hope?" The question was tossed carelessly over his shoulder. "You are still an impressionable young girl, and my son seems to have a mesmerizing effect on even sophisticated women. He did give me his word."

Darcy flushed uncomfortably. "Cullen has always been a perfect gentleman, sir. I didn't mean to imply . . . I just meant that no brother could have been more solicitous—"

Sir Laurence turned around so swiftly that Darcy jumped, startled. "A servant is waiting to show you to your room," he said. "We can discuss your future later. For now, I would merely like to point out to you that all young girls become infatuated with unsuitable men. It is a part of the rite of passage into womanhood."

There was amusement in his glance as well as something Darcy was unable to define but which made her lower her gaze and turn for the door. She had one hand on the brass knob when Sir Laurence called after her.

"I take it that none of your mother's relatives ever attempted to get in touch with you?"

Darcy shook her head. She was bewildered by the question, for Sir Laurence must have known that her mother's family had disowned her when the aristocratic Regine D'Arcy ran away with a penniless English orphan. Although Darcy did not remember her father—his ship had been lost while she was still a baby—she knew John Sinclair must have been constantly amazed at his good fortune in capturing the beautiful Regine for his bride.

"I'm not sure my mother's family in France are even aware of my existence," Darcy said. "Mother never communicated with them after she ran away."

"Dinner will be at eight. Dress formally. We shall have guests. The village seamstress will be here tomorrow, and we can discuss your new wardrobe then."

Darcy was hardly aware of his parting instructions. As she went out into the hall and followed the waiting servant girl up the great oak staircase, she pondered Sir Laurence's not-so-subtle warning about Cullen. Why, she wondered, did her guardian feel his son was so unsuitable? Or was it that she, Darcy Sinclair, was not worthy to be the wife of his heir? Suits of armor, standing like grey sentinels in the alcoves, seemed to mock her silently for her thoughts of Cullen. She longed for him to be near.

An intricately wrought tapestry hung on the wall outside the door the servant had opened. Darcy paused to admire the tapestry before following the girl into spacious but somewhat gloomy chambers.

"Would you open the draperies, please?" Darcy asked, shivering despite the fire blazing in the hearth. A four-poster bed hidden behind velvet curtains dominated the room. It stood upon a dais like an outsized throne.

When the girl did not respond, Darcy repeated her request. The girl smiled vacantly and gestured toward the portmanteau she had carried.

"Ah, I see," Darcy said. The servant was deaf and mute. The gesture asked Darcy if she wanted the portmanteau unpacked. "No—thank you. I'll do it." Darcy shook her head and smiled again, reaching out to pat the girl reassuringly on her outstretched hand.

After several futile gestures and much nodding, smiling, and pointing on Darcy's part, she was able to convince the girl that she had no further need of her services. Later Darcy would wonder at the choice of a deaf and mute servant, but at that moment she was too eager to open the carved jewel box that stood on the dressing table.

Her fingers caressed the satin-smooth wood for a moment, trying to recapture the distant image of her mother. The memory of her mother ransacking the box in search of a particular piece of jewelry came spinning down the years and with it a tear. Darcy lifted the lid and saw that the velvet tray separating the two compartments had faded with time. Several rings and two pairs of earrings lay in the upper tray. Darcy recognized one of the rings as the simple gold band that John Sinclair had given his bride. She quickly raised the tray to examine what lay in the main compartment of the jewel box. Her attention was caught immediately by a gold locket that shared a slender chain with a striking medallion. Carefully drawing the chain from amid a tangle of necklaces, Darcy held the locket on the palm of her hand. Her heart had begun to pound slowly, loudly. A coat of arms had been etched onto the beaten silver of the medallion. Although most of the details had been worn away by time, a large bird with wings outstretched as though in flight was visible in the center.

The same proud creature was worked into the gold of the locket, and touching it lightly with her fingertip, Darcy felt the locket spring open. The oil-painted miniature inside was remarkably well preserved and clear. Darcy recognized the mocking smile and black-as-night hair instantly. She was staring at the unmistakable likeness of Captain Stede Winslow.

Chapter Three

"I OWE YOU my life, m'sieur," the young Frenchman said, offering his hand to Stede Winslow in the English fashion, although a traditional French embrace seemed to be in order. "I am forever indebted to you. But surely it is dangerous to linger here at the inn?"

Stede pushed a tankard of ale across the table. "Drink, Philippe, then enjoy the meal Violet will bring. We are safe here for the time being. The Excise men found what they were seeking, and they won't return until they are informed that there is more contraband at the inn. Tell me, do you wish me to obtain a horse for you so that you may continue your journey?"

Philippe grimaced slightly at the unexpectedly bitter taste of the English ale. He was a seemingly frail youth with fair hair and light blue eyes. A cane was propped against the table beside him and when he walked he relied heavily upon its support.

"You will be able to ride?" Stede asked, trying to keep the pity out of his voice.

The china-blue eyes flashed defensively. "In the saddle, m'sieur, I have no need of my withered foot."

"I'm sorry you had to spend the night aboard my ship," Stede said quickly. "I expect you were convinced you were about to be blown to kingdom come. It was necessary, however, as I knew the Excise men would search the inn, and I didn't want you to catch a stray pistol ball."

"How did you know this?"

"They have an informer." Stede picked up his own tankard as Violet came into the room carrying a tray. She leaned forward over the table to place the food in front of Stede first, dimples appearing in her cheeks and her eyes flashing an unmistakable invitation. Stede grinned at her and winked slowly.

When she turned to give Philippe his plate she said, "And how's the young gent today? Never saw anyone sleep all day *and* all night before."

"*Mon Dieu*," Philippe said. "I lost a whole day?" He began to cough and covered his mouth with his monogrammed handkerchief.

Stede reached out casually to pat Violet's departing bottom, eliciting a giggle from her. "Even revolutionaries must sleep sometime, Philippe."

Philippe sighed. "I am not a revolutionary. I am a man of letters."

"You are a paradox, my friend. A French *aristo* who sides with the peasants . . . to the point of almost losing his own life in their cause, it seems. Certainly your radical views cost you your birthright, your liberty, and your health."

"Their cause is just, m'sieur. Surely you—an American so recently baptized in the fires of revolution yourself—must know that the old order will only give way to the new through a bloodbath."

Stede's glance was filled with compassion as he looked at the wasted body seated across from him at the rough wooden table. Despite his fragile body, Philippe's tortured eyes blazed with the fire of his ideals. Stede had found Philippe slowly dying in a prison cell he had shared with a distant Winslow relative, a cousin who languished there as a result of *lettres de cachet* unjustly condemning him to death for treason without benefit of a trial.

"Your French cousin—whom you smuggled across the Channel with me," Philippe said. "He has already departed?"

"Yesterday."

"And you stayed because of my—indisposition. I must apologize for delaying you. I realize that every minute you linger here is dangerous for you."

"Danger is the spice of life, Philippe. Tell me, what of you— will you join my cousins and the other expatriates in London? Although, strictly speaking, you are not one of them, are you, since you choose to side with the proletariat."

"I had hoped . . . I wondered—" Philippe toyed with the food on his plate. "My father is of the old order. A marquis. He disowned me when I was imprisoned for writing revolutionary pamphlets. My mother is dead. I have no one . . . I thought perhaps there would be a place for me in your country."

"My country has nothing but space. But—forgive me, what would you do there? How would you support yourself?"

"You have newspapers, do you not? Periodicals? I would do what I have always done—write. My command of your language is good. Besides, I hear there are many French settlements where I could perhaps write in my own language."

"If you would care to wait a few weeks, you could return to America with me," Stede said thoughtfully. "I'm sure we could find something for a young man of your dedication. I have unfinished business across the Channel, but when it is done . . ."

Philippe's sad countenance brightened visibly. "I would like very much to travel with you, Captain Winslow."

"Stede."

"Stede—yes. But must you return to France? Surely it will soon be too late. I could not help but overhear your conversation with your cousin. I received the impression that the woman you wish to bring out of the country is unwilling to leave."

"Nevertheless, I must make one more attempt."

Philippe shook his head wonderingly. "I thought we French were the only race who risked everything for *l'amour*."

Stede frowned slightly, his eyes deepening in color. He rose abruptly from the table. "It's almost dark, and I shall be leaving shortly. Violet will take care of you while I'm gone. There is nothing for you to fear; you are not a fugitive in England. Of course, I would prefer that you not speak of my activities to anyone."

Philippe struggled to his feet, extending his hand again and clasping Stede's fingers in a surprisingly firm grip. "They could burn off my other foot and I would not betray you. I shall never rest until I have repaid my debt to you, Stede Winslow."

"I doubt that you'll be called upon to make such a dramatic gesture on my behalf," Stede said gently. "I'm only wanted for smuggling wines and spirits on this side of the Channel. At least until I settle an old score with Sir Laurence Tregarth . . . but that's a different story."

The hayloft was damp and cold. Corinne Dubois, personal maid to the comtess, snuggled closer to the man beside her. Her cold fingers crept under his linen shirt to caress the taut flesh beneath. He murmured in his sleep, and the name he whispered was not hers. Angrily she sat up and struck his chest with a closed fist.

Stede opened his eyes warily.

"You whisper another woman's name," Corinne said fiercely. "After telling me it is I you love."

She raised her fist to strike him again, and Stede's arms went around her, pulling her back into his embrace. "The name of my ship, *cherie*. It must have been the name of my ship . . . what name did I say?"

"Oh! You try to trick me. . . ." Corinne struggled, her bosom brushing enticingly across his chest.

Stede quickly rolled her on to her back, holding her down with the weight of his body. "You are the loveliest creature in all of France. . . ."

Sharp white teeth sank into his shoulder. This was accompanied by a stream of unladylike curses.

"*Dieu!*" Stede said. "What did I say? My French does fail me on occasion—but I was sure I was paying you a compliment. Perhaps actions will speak louder than words." His mouth found hers.

"You are a fiend—a devil—and I hate you. You come here only to use me. How many times must I tell you? The comtess sees no one. She has not left her room in the chateau since the comte died. You are wasting your time, Stede Winslow." But his gentle caress was too persuasive to resist, and it wasn't long before Corinne's anger evaporated. Her words became breathless, seductive and soft as down.

"You promised to get me into the comtess's chambers," he reminded her. "You cannot be jealous of her, surely? She is an old lady."

"But somehow I think you wish to see the comtess only to find out about the other one whose name you say in your sleep."

Stede stopped that dangerous line of thought with his mouth, kissing her until she forgot everything but the tingling of her senses. She sighed. She loved him even if he did not love her in the same way. She would take him to the comtess's chambers today.

Lying beside her in the damp hay, Stede waited for the dawn to break and thought dispassionately about his self-imposed exile. He belonged to that vast and sparsely settled land across the Atlantic despite his English father and French mother. There had been times when he had regretted returning to the intrigues of Europe, but he had made a deathbed vow.

His uncle, Jean-Paul Durey—like his father, Geoffrey Winslow—had been a soldier. Both were from a long line of soldiers, and, more than once, they had fought on opposing sides in the interminable wars between their two countries. Unlike Geoffrey Winslow, a commoner who had earned his commission on the battlefield, Jean-Paul's titled father had, in the manner of French nobility, purchased his son's commission.

Geoffrey's marriage to Jean-Paul's sister had been brief, ending nine months after it had begun with Jean-Paul's sister dead and a squalling infant in her place.

"But he brought the roses to her cheeks for a little while," Jean-Paul had sighed. "He had that same quality you possess, Stede. He was so vital and full of energy that everyone around him came alive too. And he never let your mother know that he was pining away with love for his cousin, Regine D'Arcy—whose own mother, you see, was a Winslow. Still, after my sister died, the affair flaired up again. Regine was promised to an old man, chosen for her by the king himself. She could not bear it. She and Geoffrey ran away. He came to me and begged me to care for you until he could send for you. You were an infant, and he feared for your safety on a long sea voyage . . . but alas, I never saw him again. My own poor wife was barren and died before you were scarcely out of infancy.

So I brought you to the New World. We never put down roots, *mon neveu*, but life has not been too bad for us, eh?"

Jean-Paul never explained why he had departed from both his regiment and his beloved France so abruptly. Since he had never returned to his native land, Stede concluded that a scandal of some sort kept his uncle in exile.

Life had been a succession of journeys. Brief sojourns here and there, supported by various occupations. Plantation steward, riding master, bodyguard, language tutor. Until Jean-Paul became restless and bored.

When the American Revolution began, Jean-Paul was one of the first to volunteer for the continental army. Stede followed him as soon as he was tall enough to enlist. He was not yet fourteen years old.

To Stede, life was a continuing journey. Like Jean-Paul, he always yearned to know what lay beyond the next horizon. When the war ended, they resumed their nomadic existence. Jean-Paul grew quarrelsome with age. Stede tried to keep his uncle out of brawls, saw that he ate regularly, and listened patiently to an old man's ramblings.

When they brought Jean-Paul's broken body home to die, the first rumblings of revolution in France were being heard across the Atlantic.

"Promise me, you will return to France," Jean-Paul gasped out the words, the rattle of death already in his throat. "Your grandparents—cousins . . . we have many relatives. They are *aristos*, Stede. My father was a marquis. They will be torn to pieces by the mob. Listen to me, I was a soldier in the service of His Majesty—I understand these things. But the others, they know only court intrigue and the petty jealousies and power plays of the ruling classes. They do not realize what will become of them when the peasants rise up in revolt."

"Save your strength, Uncle," Stede whispered, fighting desperately to control his emotions as a grey pallor spread across Jean-Paul's swarthy skin.

"You must go back . . . help them to escape to England. A short journey across the Channel and they will be safe. Noble blood flows in your veins, Stede . . . it is your sworn duty. Promise me, swear to me a sacred oath. . . ."

Jean-Paul's eyes were glazed, but he strove valiantly to cling to life. "One . . . last . . . warning—Stede—in England you must beware—" His hands clutched at Stede and he lay panting for a moment.

"Tregarth," he said at last, as though choking on the name. "The Tregarth family of Channel Castle in Cornwall. Sworn enemies of all Winslows. An old feud, Stede. I kept . . . papers—a strong box . . . for when I die. All you must know is there."

The key to the strong box hung from a chain about Jean-Paul's neck. He had worn it for so long that Stede had long ago stopped asking why. The strong box had been left for safekeeping with a friend in Philadelphia, a physician named Vedel.

There were yellowing documents in the box. A clipping from a news sheet that told briefly of the loss of a ship on the treacherous reefs of the Bahamas. A list of the dead and missing followed. Someone had underlined the last name on the list. *Winslow, Geoffrey—passenger.*

Attached to the clipping was a letter faded with age.

"I was one of the crew, and I survived the wreck," Stede read. "Your brother-in-law was dead before we went aground, his body thrown to the sharks. The man who did it was lost, but the real murderer walks free—the sailor who killed Geoffrey Winslow while he slept was paid to do it by Sir Laurence Tregarth of Channel Castle in Cornwall. How do I know this? I refused the job myself and foolishly believed the other crewmen would do likewise. The captain did not know what happened—the storm hit us the next day. I dare not tell you who I am for fear that you will implicate me in the murder, but my conscience forces me to tell you that Geoffrey Winslow died by the will of Sir Laurence Tregarth, if not by his hand."

The remainder of the letter was illegible. Stede turned the page over and found a note in his uncle Jean–Paul's handwriting. "Stede, when you find this don't judge me too harshly. You'll wonder why I left France without investigating this accusation. Believe me, it was necessary. You see, I too was a prisoner of Regine D'Arcy's incredible allure. The king had arranged a marriage between us, and when she ran off with Geoffrey Winslow the heartache and humiliation was too much to bear, so I left France and spent my life trying to run away from my own feelings. I was desperately afraid that if I searched for the true cause of your father's death, wounds that had barely begun to heal would be wrenched open—the dull ache transformed once again into searing pain. Besides, what proof was there? Only the word of a common sailor. But Sir Laurence and your father had been rivals; there was bad blood between them. And, of course, the motive was obviously. . . ." The note ended here, and Stede could find no continuation.

He turned to the other items Dr. Vedel had stored for him. A medallion bearing the family crest, some gold coins, a family tree. Stede paid little attention to any of these things as his attention was caught by a leather tube about two feet long. After unrolling the carefully wrapped canvas within, Stede had gazed, transfixed, at the portrait of a beautiful woman.

Her eyes glowed like golden lamps, mesmerizing him. They bewitched, challenged, teased, mocked . . . they were alive. Several seconds passed before Stede was aware of a mass of tawny hair, a provocative mouth, a tip–tilted nose and smoothly rounded shoulders that drooped slightly under the weight of a handsome necklace. A pair of pale hands seemed to be expressing the restlessness of the spirit even in repose.

There was no clue to the identity of the woman, only the name of the artist—Etienne—and his title for the portrait. He had called it *Tawny Rose*.

Stede had a miniature of his mother, a dark-haired beauty with grey eyes. Jean–Paul had described his deceased wife often enough for Stede to know that she had been plump with black eyes and black hair. Clearly, the woman in the portrait was neither Jean–Paul's sister nor his wife. When Stede sailed for France, he impulsively took the portrait with him.

Jean–Paul's bequest of the long-kept gold coins financed Stede's return to France and the purchase of a small schooner. Expenses were met by the simple expediency of transporting French wines and spirits to Cornish innkeepers. At the same time, he helped his French relatives flee the peasant mobs.

He was fulfilling his promise to Jean–Paul but impatient to start a quest of his own—that of finding his father's murderer. And, unbidden, his thoughts turned frequently to the portrait.

Sometimes he awoke in the night thinking about the woman with the amber eyes. What had she been to Jean–Paul? Why had he never shown the portrait to anyone? She must now be an old woman, as Jean–Paul had been an old man. Or had the portrait been acquired, somehow, in the twilight of his life?

Stede found himself comparing real women to the woman in the picture, always to the disadvantage of the former. When the portrait came alive to haunt him, he would tell himself that no sane man fell in love with a ghost. Nevertheless, the liaisons he formed were usually with women who reminded him, in some way, of the Tawny Rose. And he hung her portrait in his cabin.

Stede watched the grey dawn send tentative fingers of light through the cracks in the weathered boards of the hayloft. Corinne was asleep again, her hair a dusky cloud over her face. You're beautiful, Corinne, but you're not my tawny rose.

He shook her gently. "Wake up, *cherie*. You will be missed at the chateau if you do not return before they awaken."

She stirred, grumbling sleepily.

"I'll come to the tradesmen's entrance in two hours. Corinne, are you listening? You will take me to the comtess's chambers?"

"I hate you, Stede Winslow," she muttered crossly. "But I will take you to the old lady."

Chapter Four

SEATED AT THE opposite end of the long dining table from Sir Laurence, Darcy felt the eyes of the guests observing her over wine glass rims and fluttering fans.

All of the men were hard–eyed and authoritative. Their women were bejeweled and sophisticated. Names and faces had blurred. Between extravagant courses, the conversation was about local politics and the problem of keeping "free traders" at bay along the thinly populated coastline.

Although Darcy's attempts to join in the conversation were met with polite responses, she felt gauche in her schoolgirl dress, which was high-necked and full-sleeved. She was relieved when the ladies retired to the drawing room, leaving the gentlemen to their brandy and cigars.

Her relief was short-lived. A petite and exquisitely lovely woman moved to her side and examined her gown with a faintly amused smile. The woman had a translucent complexion and fiery auburn hair that shone like burnished copper. She had eyes of palest green enhanced by curling lashes that were startlingly dark. Darcy was not aware that the woman had dramatized her eyes with kohl. She was dazzled by a magnificent gown of pale yellow and matching ostrich-plumed fan.

"So you are Sir Laurence's protégé." The voice was a bored drawl that marred the vision of loveliness. A voice that said its owner was already world weary despite her tender years. "We have been looking forward to meeting you."

"Forgive me . . . I know we were introduced, but—" Darcy began.

"Lady Evadne Dunforth." The woman studied Darcy coldly.

"Are you a friend of Cullen's, Lady Evadne?"

Lady Evadne's fan fluttered up over her mouth to conceal her obvious amusement at this question. Darcy waited with some discomfort for the woman to compose herself.

An older woman, resplendent in a white satin gown the exact color of her hair, had seated herself nearby. Now she leaned forward and said to Darcy, "Evadne is going to marry Cullen Tregarth."

Darcy blinked. The room faded from view for a moment, then returned. The sound of conversation, the tinkle of glasses, the roar of the flames in the hearth all continued as though Darcy's world had not been shattered by this dreadful announcement.

Somehow she was able to live through the rest of the evening without succumbing to the avalanche of tears she felt welling up inside. Later, alone in the massive four-poster bed with the curtains closed against the prying eyes of the night, Darcy soaked her pillow.

They had never had a chance. Cullen thought of her as an inexperienced schoolgirl, not as a woman. He had never seen her anywhere but at the Grafton School, the local tea shops, and the park. Once he had taken her to the zoo. All very childish pursuits. If only he could have seen her presiding over dinner at Tregarth Hall.

The image of the petite and lovely Evadne rose in Darcy's mind. Evadne was the kind of woman every man dreamed of taking as his wife. Tiny, clinging, dependent. Darcy had noticed the change in Evadne's manner the moment the men came into the drawing room. The green-eyed beauty had hung onto every word uttered by a member of the opposite sex. Undoubtedly, her bored and petulant tone was for other women.

Sighing, Darcy lay on her damp pillow, wishing she had not

grown so tall. Tiny women had all the advantages. Miss Blenning had clucked disapprovingly every time the hem of Darcy's dress inched up over her ankles, signaling another spurt of growth. Darcy had never really worried about her height before, for Cullen was a head and shoulders taller than she, and what did it matter if other men were not? Now, she thought it wasn't only a question of her height . . . she would never be able to assume that adoring, wide-eyed admiration with which Lady Evadne devastated every male. More than once, Miss Blenning had warned Darcy that young ladies should stop and think before expressing an unpopular view. In Miss Blenning's opinion, an unpopular view was one that brought a frown to male countenances. Gentlemen did not like outspoken young misses, and unfortunately Darcy had no acting abilities when it came to concealing her feelings and opinions.

In the wee hours of her first night at Tregarth Hall, Darcy was painfully aware of all of her shortcomings. Was it any wonder Cullen had chosen the delightful Evadne?

At length, unable to sleep, Darcy climbed down from the four-poster bed and pulled a dressing gown over her nightgown. She opened the door and peered down the silent and shadowed landing.

Sounds broke the silence of the sleeping castle. The creaking of ancient wood, the whisper of drafts moving unlatched doors, the moaning of wind as it tried to gain entry through rattling windows. She shivered, pulled her dressing gown closer to her body, and padded silently down the stairs. She had the vague idea that she would find the kitchen and warm some milk to help her sleep. At the foot of the stairs she became confused and could not remember the direction of the servants' quarters. A labyrinth of corridors and halls spread from the central hall like a giant spider's web.

A thin beam of light came from beneath a door on the other side of the entry hall and from within the room a low murmur of voices. Darcy hesitated, undecided as to whether to search for the kitchen or return to her room. Then she heard the tinkle of a woman's laughter and recognized it instantly as belonging to Evadne Dunforth.

Curious, Darcy thought. Evadne had departed with the other guests. At least, Evadne had thanked her host and made an elaborate show of saying good-bye to everyone before climbing into her carriage and disappearing into the night.

Darcy was about to climb the stairs again when the door across the hall suddenly opened. In a moment of panic, Darcy flung herself around the banister and into the sheltering shadows beneath the staircase. Crouching in her hiding place, she was astonished when Evadne emerged from the room, followed by Sir Laurence Tregarth.

The two silhouettes moved toward the front doors and Darcy saw Sir Laurence help Evadne with her cape. He pulled the hood up over the auburn ringlets and tied the strings with a possessive flourish. Then, to Darcy's amazement, he gathered Lady Evadne into his arms, bent her backward and kissed her mouth slowly, deliberately, and very thoroughly. Even from across the hall, Darcy could almost feel the passion of the kiss. Blushing, she looked away.

A moment later she heard the door close and Sir Laurence's footsteps coming across the flagged hall toward the staircase. Terrified that he would see her, she shrank back under the stairs, trying to stifle the thudding of her heart.

Boots paused at the foot of the stairs for a split second; then, the staircase creaked over her head.

She remained in her hiding place for several minutes after the sound of Sir Laurence's footsteps had faded. Cullen's fiancée and his father. Sir Laurence and Lady Evadne. At first, Darcy was elated that Evadne did not really care for Cullen. Cullen would never share a woman with his father. Then Darcy realized with dismay that their secret meeting must mean that neither intended that Cullen or anyone else know of their relationship. And Darcy could not possibly tell him.

Creeping back up the stairs to her room, Darcy wondered

about a woman who while betrothed to one man could kiss another in that shameless way. The girls at the Grafton School had heard about courtesans, the most dangerous sort of woman of all. Was that what Evadne was? Darcy fell asleep with hope and despair battling in her mind.

The days sped by in a confusion of activity. There was much to learn about running a large household. The butler and the housekeeper kept Darcy busy from morning until night. Both were rather dour individuals who did not try to disguise the fact that they considered Darcy too young to be mistress of Tregarth Hall.

A seamstress came from the village, and Darcy spent hours being fitted for new clothes. Time was allotted for riding lessons. Sir Laurence pointed out tersely that the type of riding she had done in London—a leisurely canter along Rotten Row —would hardly suffice in the rough terrain of Cornwall.

There were dinner parties every night, and Darcy was dismayed to learn that Sir Laurence was postponing the "real" entertaining until Darcy was properly clothed and trained for it.

Darcy quickly learned that she had one ally in the vast and terrifying household. The mute servant girl, whose name was Gwyneth, was always at Darcy's elbow ready to guide her. Despite her crowded hours, Darcy took a few minutes each day to begin teaching Gwyneth to read and write. The girl was bright, exceptionally so, as though nature had compensated for the loss of her hearing by giving her a brain more nimble than most. Darcy wrote "apple" in one of her old exercise books, then showed Gwyneth a shiny red apple from the barrel in the pantry. Laboriously Gwyneth copied the word, nodding and smiling.

From discreet questions to the butler and housekeeper, Darcy was able to determine that Cullen's engagement to Lady Evadne had not yet been officially announced. All of the present staff of servants had been hired within the year since Sir Laurence had returned from abroad. Before that, the castle had stood unused for years in the care of an estate steward. Renovations and restoration, however, had begun years ago . . . in fact, about a year after Sir Laurence married Darcy's mother.

"But is it definite," Darcy asked the housekeeper, "that Cullen is going to marry Lady Evadne?" She hoped her tone did not betray her true feelings in the matter.

The housekeeper's deep-set eyes glittered darkly at the question. "Well . . ." she sniffed slightly. "Lady Evadne seems to think so."

Darcy had been at Tregarth Hall for almost a month when word came that Cullen was on his way home from France. She counted the days until his return, each morning trying on all of her new gowns to determine which was the most becoming. Gwyneth's nimble fingers coaxed Darcy's hair into a pompadour despite Darcy's refusal to pad her locks in the fashion of the day, and Darcy felt less like a schoolgirl each time she surveyed her reflection in the mirror. After all, she did have interesting eyes.

Telling herself that Cullen was betrothed to another and that she could hope for no more than a sisterly relationship with him did little to diminish Darcy's eagerness for his return.

As it happened, she was out riding when Cullen arrived. Her riding master had put horse and rider through their paces with a vengeance. Darcy's riding habit clung damply to her back and her hair straggled limply about her shoulders. She was absolutely certain her nose was shining like a beacon. Cullen was standing at the foot of the staircase talking with his father as she entered the hall. The familiar black-eyed glance stopped her breath in her throat.

"Darcy!" Cullen exclaimed, his handsome features breaking into a pleased smile.

Darcy wanted to fling herself into his arms but contented herself with outstretched hands instead, which he caught in a reassuringly warm grasp. The hooded gaze of Sir Laurence flickered over the two of them in a speculative manner.

"Did you have a good journey?" Darcy asked, feasting her

eyes on the chiseled features and romantic dark eyes. Cullen's dark brown hair waved about his brow and his queue curled thickly at the nape of his neck. He had always scorned the practice of wearing a wig.

"Tiresome would better describe it," Cullen said. "The insolence of the lower classes in France is becoming unbelievable. I'm glad to be back where we know how to deal with riffraff." Under his father's watchful gaze, he released her hands. "Tell me, what do you think of the ancestral home? A bit different from the Grafton School, wouldn't you say?"

"It's awe inspiring," Darcy said. "I still don't know my way around."

"I made Father promise not to show you the dungeons until I arrived," Cullen said.

Darcy shuddered. "I think the wine cellars are gloomy. Are there really dungeons?"

"Of course. Tregarth Hall was once a castle. Hadn't you noticed?"

"There will be time enough for small talk later," Sir Laurence interrupted. "I suggest you both go and dress for dinner. Cullen, Evadne will be here shortly. When you're dressed, you could wait for her in the drawing room so that you may have your reunion in private."

Watching Cullen's expression, Darcy was sure she saw a brief flash of defiance in the glance he gave his father. She hesitated, hoping Cullen would make some comment, but he did not. All the way up to her room the word "reunion" echoed in her mind.

Evadne looked utterly bewitching at dinner. She wore a jade green gown trimmed with swans' down, and the perfectly matched stones about her throat and adorning her delicate ears surely represented a fortune in emeralds. Darcy was sure that much of her mother's jewelry was imitation, but there was a topaz pendant to wear with the gown of gold-colored silk she had chosen. She was surprised to find that Evadne was the only guest for dinner.

Cullen's eyes lit up when she entered the dining room. He rose instantly and waved the footman away from her chair. "You look charming, Darcy. That gown is a far cry from the school dresses I remember. It makes you look like a sleek lioness—all tawny mane of hair and golden eyes. It's a good thing there are no susceptible young swains present. They wouldn't be able to take their eyes off you."

Evadne's eyes flashed ominously, and Darcy expected a sharp comment, but before Evadne could unsheath her claws, Sir Laurence said, "I see you are wearing one of your mother's necklaces. Good. She had some fine old pieces. Tell me, did you find the locket and medallion? I have been expecting you to mention them and was surprised when you did not."

"I did wonder about them," Darcy said. "But I was afraid . . . I mean—" She broke off, sorry she had spoken.

"You were afraid you had discovered a skeleton from your mother's past when you saw the locket that contained a picture that was neither of your father nor of me," Sir Laurence finished for her. His expression was amused in a supercilious way.

Darcy looked down at her hands, concentrating on placing her linen serviette smoothly upon her lap.

"Who is . . . was the man in the miniature?" she asked.

"A ruffian best forgotten," Sir Laurence said. "I wanted you to see his likeness, however, because we believe his son is one of the smugglers plaguing us. The man in the miniature ruined your mother's life. If you see someone resembling him, guard your honor well. The Winslows are unscrupulous seducers."

"Winslow?" Darcy repeated, reaching for her water goblet with shaking fingers.

"Your mother never told you of him?"

"No." Her mother had told Darcy about John Sinclair, her father. So many stories of his kind and steadfast heart. Regine had never spoken of any other man, at least not one with the name of Winslow.

"Let's not cast a pall over my homecoming, Father," Cullen

said lightly. "You know you always get angry and make everyone's life unbearable when you think of the Winslows."

"And tonight is such a happy occasion," Evadne bubbled, gazing adoringly at Cullen. "To have our dearest Cullen safely home again."

Cullen's expression did not mirror her joy. Again Darcy felt a flicker of hope. He was not in love with Evadne. Darcy was sure of it.

The liveried footmen served the last course of the meal, a tray of assorted cheeses and fresh fruit, and withdrew. As soon as they were alone, Sir Laurence leaned forward. Darcy felt a twinge of apprehension as the piercing eyes rested on her.

"We might as well take care of all the family business tonight," he said. "Next month we shall have Darcy's coming-out ball, followed in short order by the party to announce the engagement."

Evadne simpered and lowered her eyes while Cullen squirmed uncomfortably in his chair, avoiding everyone's glance.

"Cullen and Evadne are to be married, Darcy. As you will also marry in due course. However, you will have ample time to accustom yourself to the idea. You will live at Tregarth Hall and learn to run a large household in preparation for your marriage."

Darcy listened to Sir Laurence's recital with a numb sense of foreboding. His voice was as impersonal as if he were discussing the mating of one of the mares in his stable. She felt a surge of anger. It was, of course, common practice for fathers to arrange their daughters' marriages. But Sir Laurence was not her father. Out of the corner of her eye she saw that Cullen had downed several glasses of wine in quick succession.

"And may I ask," Darcy said at last, her color rising, "If you have already chosen my husband-to-be?"

The hooded eyes regarded her opaquely. "We have lived abroad many years, Darcy, as you know. No one here in Cornwall knew of my marriage to your mother. I believe it best if we do not mention the fact. Not that it would make the forthcoming marriage illegal—but there is no point in giving rise to unnecessary gossip.''

''I'm not sure what you mean . . . what has my mother's marriage to you to do with the marriage you have arranged for me?''

''Because, my dear,'' Sir Laurence replied softly, leaning forward to watch her reaction, ''You will become Lady Tregarth. I intend to marry you myself.''

Chapter Five

THERE WAS TIME to plan an escape she told herself when her first panic at Sir Laurence's announcement had subsided. The weddings were to be in the spring; first Cullen's, then a quiet ceremony for Sir Laurence and herself. By then Darcy would be far away. Where, exactly, she was not sure. At the back of her mind was the unquenchable hope that Cullen would run away with her.

During the busy days before her coming-out ball, Darcy felt that Cullen avoided her. She longed to talk with him as she had in the days when he visited her at school. They had confided in each other then, expressing their hopes and fears freely. She wondered sadly what had become of the dashing and debonair young man who had vowed to spend his life in the pursuit of pleasure. The romantic ideal of the Grafton schoolgirls was behaving like a country squire. Worse, he seemed to shrink in the presence of his father.

On the day before the ball, Cullen came upon Darcy in the kitchens giving last-minute instructions to the cook and scullery maids.

"Father wants me to choose the wines for dinner," he said. "While I'm going down to the wine cellars, I thought it would be a good opportunity to show you the dungeons."

Darcy's heart gave an odd little lurch.

He led the way down the stone steps that over the centuries had been deeply indented by thousands of footsteps. Darcy wondered how many of those feet had been destined for the dungeons rather than the wine cellars. She shivered and reached out her hand unconsciously toward Cullen's retreating back. He stopped, the lantern held high, and turned to look at her over his shoulder. "What is it?" he asked.

The flickering light played tricks with his features, the shadows etching into his face the same satanic lines that made his father's countenance so sinister. Darcy felt an unexpected wave of fear as the familiar became suddenly unfamiliar.

"Nothing. It's just so gloomy."

"Watch your step, there is always water down here. It seeps in from the sea, and the stones are slippery," Cullen said as they turned at the foot of the steps in the opposite direction of the wine cellars. At the end of a long corridor was another door, heavily studded and iron-barred, and beyond it another flight of stone steps.

A musty odor, rank and clinging, rose to greet them. Darcy stifled a scream as a grey shadow scurried down the steps before the lantern's beam of light.

"Rats were the least of the problems of the poor devils who were imprisoned here," Cullen remarked. He placed the lantern on a cobweb-shrouded table in the center of a large room flanked by doors. "Each of those doors leads to a cell where prisoners who warranted private quarters were kept. The rest were manacled to the wall over there. You can see that the iron rings are still attached to the stones. That fearsome contraption behind you is a rack, and that table over there with all of the rusty implements on it holds such delightful diversions as thumbscrews, facemasks, branding irons. . . ."

"Stop!" Darcy said quickly. "I'd rather not hear. Why does Sir Laurence keep all these dreadful implements of torture?"

"It amuses him. When I was a small boy living abroad with him he always promised me that some day we would return in triumph to Tregarth Hall and restore it to its former glory. Now that I'm actually here, I wonder why we wanted the place badly enough to . . ."

"To what, Cullen?" Darcy prompted as he paused.

"Nothing. To come back here after all this time. Darcy, you have turned into a beautiful woman. Quite breathtaking, in fact. You were always a compelling child, but now that you're out of those ghastly school clothes. . . ."

They were standing close together and almost without thinking Darcy took the short step into his arms. She felt his hands encircle her waist, pulling her into a bone-crushing embrace. She was surprised at his strength in view of the lethargic air of boredom and compliance he had affected since his return from France. A moment later his lips grazed hers experimentally. She closed her eyes and allowed her body to relax against his, feeling the buttons of his jacket dig into her flesh through the thin material of her dress.

His mouth closed over hers, his tongue forcing entry between her teeth. She loved him so much that it seemed inconceivable for his kiss to fill her with a cold sense of shame. In the outer reaches of her consciousness she rationalized that she had so longed for this moment that the reality was bound to be less than the dream. She was inexperienced in the art of love, and there was no doubt that kissing was an activity that required the cooperation of both partners. Therefore, the failure of the kiss must be blamed on herself, never her beloved Cullen.

When he released her lips she opened her eyes and looked up at him. "I love you, Cullen. I've loved you for so long I don't know when it began . . . or how it can end."

"Darcy, you're so excitingly beautiful, and I want you so much. But we must be careful. Father has gone to the village today to speak with the Excise men about catching the free traders. Evadne is having her ball gown fitted, so we shall be safe for a little while."

"But . . ." Darcy said, her face stricken, "Are you really going to marry her? Now that we've discovered we love each other, why don't you just tell your father—"

"Darcy, no! Father told me years ago that you were to be his bride as soon as you came of age. But Darcy, that doesn't mean there can be no happiness for us. We shall live here under the same roof. There will be times when we can be together. Oh, my darling. . . ." His breathing was becoming more rapid, and his dark eyes were glazed with passion.

"Why did you never tell me about Evadne?"

"I hoped. . . " He paused, as though considering carefully what he was about to say. "For a way to marry you. I knew we would be penniless if we eloped. I even went to France to search for your mother's family in the hope that they would provide you with a dowry."

"So that's why you went to France," Darcy breathed. "Did you find them—my mother's family?"

"I found the chateau. The comte died some years ago. There is only the comtess, your grandmother, and she lives in seclusion, refusing to see or receive messages from anyone. They told me that her mind was unhinged and that she had never recovered from the shock of her only daughter running away with Geoffrey Winslow."

"Geoffrey Winslow? Oh, no, Cullen, you must have the name Winslow on your mind. My father was John Sinclair, an English sea captain."

Cullen's mouth hardened slightly, and Darcy noticed that in the dim light his lips appeared thin and cruel. Odd that she had never noticed this before. Perhaps because she had rarely seen him except in the daylight. Darkness certainly did not enhance his features, the shadows revealing the bones beneath the flesh.

"Captain John Sinclair was the captain of the ship boarded by your mother and Geoffrey Winslow. There was a storm, and the ship was wrecked. Did she never tell you this?"

Darcy shook her head. The oppressiveness of the torture chamber and the barred doors was beginning to chill her blood, but she was anxious to hear more about the mysterious Winslows.

"John Sinclair managed to get your mother into the longboat and eventually they were cast up on an island with a few crew members. Geoffrey Winslow was never seen or heard from again. Captain Sinclair married your mother and brought her to his home in England. Later, you were born.''

''And all those years, my mother kept a miniature of him in her locket,'' Darcy said wonderingly. She thought fleetingly of Stede Winslow, the smuggler who had come to her room at the Inn of the Blue Lantern. For the moment, she decided, it would be better not to mention him. Was he the son of Geoffrey Winslow as Sir Laurence suspected? And if so, did that mean Geoffrey had survived the shipwreck after all?

Cullen's hand slid from her back to around her waist, and he pulled her to him again. Darcy stiffened. ''Cullen, please. I hate this dreary place. Could we go back up into the daylight?''

''I'm sorry . . . it's just that you're so damned desirable. I realize that this isn't the time. You aren't ready yet, and you need time to accept things. You see, my sweet little innocent, one can't always have what one wants in life. Certain compromises are necessary. Half a loaf is better than none. You'll come to understand in time.''

Darcy shuddered, hoping he did not mean what he was saying. She pulled away from him and started back up the dripping steps so hastily that she slipped. Her knee went down on the cold stone with a painful crack and if Cullen had not caught her she would have fallen over the edge, which had no railing, to the floor below.

''You see? I warned you to be careful. You must never run away from me again. Bad fortune will surely befall you if you do.'' His tone was teasing, but Darcy's heart was thudding and she made haste to proceed up the steps and away from that evil place.

The great hall was decorated with evergreen boughs and dried flowers. A fir log of enormous size blazed in the hearth. In the adjacent banquet room, the tables groaned under the weight of the festive dishes. The chill of winter crept about the damp corridors of Tregarth Hall, and Gwyneth shook her head vigorously when Darcy took a frail taffeta gown from her wardrobe. Gwyneth pointed to a garnet-colored velvet dress.

"Perhaps you're right; the velvet would be warmer. But it isn't a ball gown. Oh, well, what does it matter? Most coming-out balls are in the summer, not the winter. And it seems strange that I should have a ball to present me to society when my future has already been decided."

Gwyneth gave her a puzzled smile.

"I would write you a note, but we haven't time. Some day I'm going to teach you to read my lips. I shall have to give the matter some thought, but I know you can do it." Darcy squeezed Gwyneth's hand. She regarded her more as a friend than as a servant, to the housekeeper's consternation and Sir Laurence's amusement.

"The girl's mother was badly frightened while she was carrying the infant in her womb," Sir Laurence told her one day. "She was accidentally locked in the torture chamber overnight. The midwives claimed that her premature labor and the baby's deafness were the result of the ordeal."

"And what became of Gwyneth's mother?" Darcy inquired.

"She died giving birth," Sir Laurence said.

Darcy was struck by the serene beauty of Gwyneth's face, with her expressive grey eyes and the tendrils of glossy brown hair that sometimes escaped from the cap she wore to proclaim her status as a servant. Gwyneth had delicate features, and her wide-set eyes were trusting and vulnerable.

Gwyneth smiled approvingly when Darcy was attired in the red velvet dress.

"Perhaps," Darcy said, studying her reflection in the mirror, "We can push the sleeves down off the shoulders a little so it will look more festive."

When she went down to stand in the receiving line, however, the sleeves covered her shoulders and her only jewelry was her mother's gold locket. The rich-colored velvet and the simple lines of the dress seemed to call for plain gold. Darcy had started to remove the miniature of Geoffrey Winslow but had stopped. Somehow, removing it seemed in opposition to her mother's wishes.

She was acutely aware of the necklace throughout the evening. The smooth gold caressed her skin and the bold blue eyes of the man whose likeness was imprisoned within the tiny heart-shaped locket seemed to encourage her to hold her head high and challenge the world.

Sir Laurence studied her for a long moment when she appeared, and Darcy was afraid he was about to order her back upstairs to change clothes. At length, a small smile curved his thin lips. "Yes. You will stand out amid the overblown blossoms in that gown. The restraint will be in sharp contrast. Very clever of you, my dear. You are fulfilling all of my hopes for you. Your riding master tells me he has never had a female pupil to equal your skill."

His approval and praise were more ominous than reassuring.

Evadne was small and fragile looking in floating white chiffon embroidered with silver threads but the effect was spoiled by a profusion of diamonds glittering coldly about her throat, on her ears, her wrists, in her hair. The glinting stones dominated the woman who wore them. Cullen was attentively at her side.

After dinner, the musicians assembled on the dais at one end of the hall, and the dancing began. The oak floor had been polished with beeswax in order to make it sufficiently slippery to allow dancing shoes to glide over the smooth surface. As the guests spilled out onto the floor for a minuet, Darcy found her hand taken firmly by Sir Laurence.

He was an accomplished if somewhat stiff dancer. His eyes never left Darcy's face, and although she usually enjoyed dancing, she felt uncomfortable under Sir Laurence's constant scrutiny. He watches me in the same manner the hunter watches his prey, Darcy thought. She avoided his eyes and fixed her gaze instead on his powdered wig whenever they passed close to one another during the dance.

More and more guests arrived until the great hall and banquet rooms were packed to overflowing. Some of the guests sat upon the stairs, balancing plates on their laps while others circled the upper gallery watching the dancing from their vantage point. Some of the candles had burned out and a few of the lamps were out of oil, but as the spirits and liqueurs were consumed no one seemed to notice the diminished light.

Just before midnight Darcy left the dance floor to speak with the housekeeper about late refreshments. Making her way along the hall towards the servants' wing, Darcy was startled when a figure stepped from behind a suit of armor in a shadowy alcove.

She recognized the flashing blue eyes and impertinent expression immediately. Her hand flew to the locket nestled against her breast as though the tiny miniature had suddenly been transformed into a flesh and blood man. "What are you doing here?" she gasped.

Captain Stede Winslow grinned and made a sweeping bow. "Mistress Sinclair. I was afraid you would never stop dancing. Why, dear lady, I'm here to see you, of course. Have I not been haunted by the memory of soft flesh and pliant lips since our first meeting?"

There was a moment's silence as they regarded each other warily, both well aware that her scream would have brought immediate aid and the capture of a fugitive. Darcy drew a deep breath. "I think you had better leave. I gather the Tregarths and Winslows are not exactly on speaking terms."

The blue eyes lit up with interest. "Ah! So you were interested enough to inquire about me. As I was interested enough in you to risk coming here tonight. An auspicious start, my love."

"I am not your love, sir. And with regard to the Winslow family, I know only that my mother was . . . enamoured . . . of a man named Geoffrey Winslow."

"Whose locket you are wearing. Tell me, what did Sir Laurence say when he saw you wearing it?"

The etching of a family crest on the locket, Darcy thought.

Was he inferring that Sir Laurence would recognize it as being the Winslow crest? The bird in flight. A bird of prey, no doubt. They had chosen the centerpiece of their crest well. It suited this bold-eyed pirate and the likeness of the man contained within the locket.

"He made no comment on such a trivial matter. I merely wore the locket tonight because I felt it complimented my gown."

"Tell me, Miss Sinclair. Do you believe in destiny?"

"If you mean do I believe our fate is written in our stars, the answer is no. I believe we make our own destinies." She was acutely aware of his physical nearness and unable to define the electric tension that made tiny nerve points tingle.

"But there is still that element of chance in our lives, don't you think? A chance encounter . . . a seemingly meaningless incident that nevertheless changes the course of our lives. Surely there is some unseen hand of fate in such matters?"

"Do you refer to our meeting at the Inn of the Blue Lantern?"

"You've been on my mind ever since. You were the one unexpected element in my plans . . . and I fear you may be my undoing."

Darcy glanced back over her shoulder, fearful that one of the footmen might be en route to the kitchen. The vague feeling persisted in the back of her mind that she was in some way protecting her mother's memory rather than a law-breaking rogue. "What do you want here? For a smuggler, you seem less cautious than your occupation demands."

Stede laughed softly. "Faint heart ne'er won a fair lady. But you're right that I must not bring disaster down upon your pretty head—at least not yet. It was an easy matter for me to slip in because of the legions of guests and I'll be gone the way I came if you'll hear me out. I came to warn you that I believe you are in grave danger."

"Danger?" Darcy repeated, able to think only of the narrow bed in the Inn of the Blue Lantern and the curious sensations the pressure of his lean body had aroused in her.

"I believe Sir Laurence killed your mother and that he intends to kill you as soon as you've served your purpose."

She staggered back, almost colliding with the suit of armor, and Stede caught her in his arms. "I'm sorry—there isn't time to lead up to the story gently. You know that revolution in France is inevitable? If your grandmother, the comtess, cannot be persuaded to leave, you could be the last of your line. You would be heir to a king's ransom in family jewels, even without the chateau and land that will surely be claimed by the new people's government. Sir Laurence Tregarth wants the D'Arcy wealth. He has always wanted it. Did you know he was one of your mother's suitors when she was young? They met before she was widowed."

"You said he killed my mother," Darcy whispered, not resisting the comforting pressure of his arms.

"You must hear the whole story—please. You see, your mother and my father were first cousins. Your grandmother was a Winslow who became the Comtess D'Arcy upon her marriage. The comte would not give permission for your mother to marry my father although they were madly in love. Regine said she would never go against her father's wishes. My father foolishly rushed into marriage with another French noblewoman—my mother—who died giving birth to me. Regine then confessed she had never stopped loving him, but it was too late because the comte had arranged a marriage to a man chosen by the king himself. Regine and my father ran away. The ship they sailed on was captained by John Sinclair, who saved your mother when they ran aground in a storm. My father perished."

"And so my mother married John Sinclair . . . my father," Darcy said. "And when he died, she married Sir Laurence. But you said he killed her. I was told she died of yellow fever."

"I met your grandmother. She told me that her first word about your mother was from Sir Laurence—that they were married and living in the West Indies. Although she wrote directly to your mother she received only letters from Sir

Laurence—and then, a chilling letter from your mother's maid, a bond servant of some education.

"She wrote saying that she had learned of the comtess's relationship to her mistress from letters on Sir Laurence's desk, and she begged your grandmother to do something to save her poor mistress from Sir Laurence's jealous rages. Even as she wrote, Regine was being forced by her husband to care for plantation hands who were dying of yellow fever. Darcy, the date on that letter was *after* Sir Laurence notified the chateau that your mother was dead. What manner of man says his wife is dead while she is still alive?"

Darcy shivered. "But perhaps she was so ill he knew death was inevitable? That is flimsy evidence on which to accuse a man."

"There was another survivor of the shipwreck," Stede said, his jaw hardening. "A sailor who wrote to my uncle telling him that my father did not perish at sea but was murdered while he slept and was tossed overboard by a man paid by Sir Laurence. Darcy, the Tregarths are notorious gamblers. Sir Laurence gambled away his own inherited wealth while he was still a young man. The comte died shortly after hearing your mother was dead. When the comtess dies, the family fortune passes into the hands of your mother's closest relative, Sir Laurence. Provided, of course, that you are no longer living. Sir Laurence had a continuing correspondence with your grandmother over the years, yet she did not know of your existence. Why?"

"But he has asked me to marry him. He kept me in a private school and intends that I learn to run Tregarth Hall. Does this sound like a man planning to kill me? How do I know you are telling me the truth? All I know about you is that you are a smuggler. Where do you fit into all of this?"

She felt him tense. The pause was brief but long enough to cast a shadow of doubt. "Apparently, your mother was an exotically magnetic woman. She cast a spell over every man who knew her, including my uncle Jean-Paul, who raised me in America. He kept a portrait of her. When I returned to France,

I traced the artist, and through him, the comtess. But I would have found her eventually even without the portrait because your grandmother was a Winslow. Darcy, for now you must believe that I am interested only in saving the life of the daughter of the woman my father loved.''

"I'm not a fool," Darcy said. "No man risks his life for such a reason. It seems more likely that you believe Sir Laurence killed your father and you wish to use me in some way to help avenge his death."

"I wouldn't use a woman against her will in the pursuit of a personal vendetta. At least tell me you'll refuse to marry Sir Laurence until you can meet your grandmother, the comtess. I am going to attempt to bring her out of France. She has resisted my efforts so far. The chateau is quite remote and has been spared the peasants' wrath so far, but it is only a matter of time before full-scale revolution sweeps France.''

They were so engrossed in their conversation that neither saw the figure that started down the corridor toward them, then, seeing Darcy's hair gleaming in the candlelight, pressed himself back against the wall. A moment later, Sir Laurence went silently back the way he came.

"Cullen told me that my grandmother's mind was unhinged," Darcy told Stede. "Did you meet her? Is it so?''

"No, it is not. She is frail, and loved her husband and daughter so much that she lost interest in life when she lost them. She is a recluse, but her mind is quicker than my own.''

"Perhaps she will come. . . ." Darcy began.

The voice cracked between them with the impact of a whip. "How dare you invade my home, you misbegotten bastard?''

They turned to look into the malevolant stare of Sir Laurence. The candlelight was mirrored in the thin blade of the rapier that was pointed toward Stede's heart.

Chapter Six

STEDE'S ARM WENT out instinctively to push Darcy out of danger. He was armed only with a sheathed knife hanging from his belt and fastened with a silver buckle bearing the Winslow crest. Leaping backward, he seized the suit of armor and sent it crashing into Sir Laurence's path. The moment's grace gave him time to unsheath his knife.

Sir Laurence laughed, a cold empty sound that sent echoes in mocking ripples down the surrounding corridors. He kicked the armor aside, making small circles with the tip of his rapier as he advanced. "Like father, like son, I see. Sneaking in back doors to press your court on ladies a cur like you cannot win in any other manner."

Deflecting the rapier with his knife, Stede side-stepped as Sir Laurence lunged. "We Winslows never took a woman against her will. Can the Tregarths say the same?"

The rapier slashed the air, and Stede ducked. On the wall behind him were a pair of crossed broadswords. Stede feinted with the knife, recklessly parrying the angry strokes of the rapier. "How appropriate that I must wield knife against sword. Was it not always thus with the house of Tregarth? No contest unless against a weaker opponent? No battle unless with superior weapons?"

"Oh, fear not. I do not intend to kill you in the presence of my intended bride." Sir Laurence glanced down the corridor. Half a dozen servants watched and waited while their master enjoyed himself, ready to charge to his aid if the duel should take a wrong turn. "But perhaps a scar or two on your face would make you less appealing."

Suddenly the rapier opened a cut over Stede's eye. Darcy screamed as blood spurted. Stede raised his knife and threw it. Surprised, Sir Laurence jumped back, only to trip over the fallen suit of armor. He went crashing to the stone-flagged floor with a shout of rage. Instantly the servants came running toward him.

Stede turned, jerking the broadswords from the wall. Holding one in each hand, he kept the first two servants at bay as he backed away from their wild lunges.

"Fetch pistols—quickly—cut off his retreat." Sir Laurence scrambled to his feet.

The two servants fell, one clutching a wound in his side and the other's sword sent hurtling from his bloodied hand as he lost his balance.

Stede grinned at Darcy, holding the two swords upright in a split-second salute. "Farewell, my lady. Until we meet again." Then he turned and raced down the corridor toward the stone steps leading to the cellars.

"After him!" Sir Laurence shouted, cursing as he was forced to detour around the fallen armor.

Darcy saw servants bringing pistols running from the opposite direction. Stepping into the entrance to the corridor down which Stede was disappearing, she crumpled to the floor in a faint, effectively blocking pursuit down the narrow passage.

Lying on the cold floor, she closed her eyes and tried not to jump as she felt something hard jab her ribs. Surreptitiously, her fingers closed around the object . . . a buckle. It must have fallen from Stede's belt. She kept it in her hand.

"Stand aside, let me get to her," said Sir Laurence's voice.

Hands went under her knees and slipped around her neck. She felt herself lifted into the air. "Get out of my way," Sir Laurence ordered. "After that man—bring him back. I'll have the lot of you whipped if he gets away."

Darcy allowed her head to hang limply over his arm, forcing

herself not to shudder at the touch of his hands and the proximity of his gaunt body.

After a few steps, they were surrounded by a different babble of voices. Guests. "What happened? Is she all right?" and, distinctly, Evadne's bored drawl. "The excitement of her first ball was no doubt too much for the poor child."

Sir Laurence said, "She has fainted. No, it's quite all right, I can manage. If you will excuse us . . . please continue the festivities. I shall return shortly."

The voices faded, and Darcy realized from the bouncing of her body and Sir Laurence's labored breathing that they were ascending the staircase. She could hear no accompanying footsteps. Surely he did not intend to carry her into her own chambers—to her bed? Oh, where was Gwyneth? The girl often seemed to have a sixth sense about Darcy's needs. She would appear as though in answer to some soundless summons while other servants ignored jangling bells.

A few minutes later Darcy was laid upon her bed. She pushed the buckle she was holding beneath the pillow.

Sir Laurence's hand went to her throat, pulling the locket from her neck with such violence that she felt the chain break. She did not allow herself to open her eyes, silently willing Gwyneth to appear.

The locket made a forlorn tinkling sound as it hit the floor. Then his hand was back, tearing at the neck of her gown. When his fingers touched the flesh beneath, she opened her eyes, trying to feign bewilderment.

"Sir Laurence," she murmured, wondering whether to add "Where am I?" but deciding against it.

He stared down at her with cold fury in his eyes. "Spare me any further theatrics." The material of her dress gave way as he continued to tug at her neckline. She gave a little cry of fright and clutched at his hands to try to stop him.

"But my dear child, this is the prescribed treatment for fainting spells," he said, giving the dress another vicious jerk. "To free the victim from restraining bonds and allow her to breathe more easily." The material was rent to the waist, exposing the chemise beneath.

Sir Laurence bent over her so that his face was inches from hers. "Did you really believe I would be taken in by your little ruse to allow the smuggler to escape? Did you dare to presume that I would not see through your ploy? My dear child, I spent years dangled on the wiles of your mother. I see now how I should have handled her. It seems the only way to deal with the women of your line is to crush their spirits. The only way to be sure your wanton caresses are not given to every passing scoundrel."

Then he was kissing her, his thin lips like cold flame, long bony fingers digging into her upper arms and pulling her toward him. She struggled, freeing her hands to beat on his chest, trying to turn her head. Where Cullen's kiss had merely been distasteful, his father's mouth brutalized her lips in a way that suggested defilement such as she dare not imagine.

"Damn you," he muttered as she tore her lips from his for a moment. "You *will* submit. I promise you." He grabbed her by the shoulders and pinned her to the bed as his mouth descended to hers. Then she felt his teeth, and somewhere in the far recesses of her mind he had been transformed into a hound from hell savaging her in some evil rite.

The door to her chambers creaked open behind them, sending in a gust of cold air from the corridor. The bed curtains fluttered, and, although no one spoke, they were aware of a presence in the room. Darcy sighed with relief as Sir Laurence released her.

"Damn you, girl, what do you want? Who sent for you?" he demanded angrily.

Darcy pushed her hair out of her eyes. Gwyneth! She silently blessed the girl as she came quickly to her mistress's side.

Seeing Gwyneth's worried eyes drop to her bodice, Darcy sat up slowly and pulled the torn velvet together. "Thank you, Gwyneth," she whispered, as though Gwyneth could hear.

Then she said in a normal voice, "Sir Laurence was just leaving. Weren't you, Sir Laurence?"

His lips compressed. "There will be time enough to teach you to obey," he said, turning on his heel to stride to the door. He looked back over his shoulder with a faint smile. "When you are Lady Tregarth."

The moment the door closed behind him, Darcy jumped off the bed and ran to pick up the locket. Snapping it open, she held the picture of Geoffrey Winslow up for Gwyneth to see. "Gwyneth . . . Captain Winslow . . . he looks like this man. Did he make good his escape? Oh, bother, how can I make you understand? Tomorrow you are going to begin to learn to read my lips."

But Gwyneth was nodding vigorously, pointing to the miniature and smiling. Darcy sighed with relief and took the silver buckle from beneath her pillow, allowing her fingers to drift over the crest, with its proud eagle beaten into the silver. She would have to return the buckle to Stede she thought with a secret glow of pleasure. He had risked his life to warn her about Sir Laurence.

Chapter Seven

CORINNE DUBOIS MOODILY placed a decanter, wine glass, and platter of tiny iced cakes upon a silver tray, then folded a linen napkin with impatient fingers. Where was that rogue, Stede Winslow?

He had promised to be back two, no, three days ago. But he had yet to appear, and Corinne's warm blood churned with need for him. She wanted to enslave him, have him grovel for her favors, yet always felt as though it were she who pursued him. If she ever found another woman in his arms, she would kill her; this she vowed each time Stede went away.

How easy it would be to destroy him. The Revolutionary Tribunal would give a great deal to know who was spiriting away *aristos* before they could be accused of crimes against the people. But Corinne wanted Stede too much to betray him.

She went slowly up to the comtess's room, wrinkling her nose with distaste as she thought of the ravages of time. The comtess was a frail old lady, unable to leave her boudoir and having no desire to be part of the world beyond her brocaded walls. Corinne alone, of all of the chateau staff, was allowed to wait upon her mistress.

Corinne hated to look at the old woman's shriveled body and be reminded that her own youth would one day fade. The old lady's mind had sharpened with the passing of the years as though to compensate for her failing body, and Corinne was sure the comtess sometimes read her mind.

She pushed open the door and, speaking in English, said,

"Here we are, Madame. Your wine and cakes. The *petits fours* —the ones you like." She always thought of her mistress as "the foreigner," for despite the comtess's fifty years in France, her French was so heavily accented as to be almost imcomprehensible, and some of her habits were still so Anglo-Saxon and gauche.

The comtess was sitting at her desk in a patch of sunlight that came through the window, writing in her journal. She closed the leather-bound book as Corinne approached. Two keys on a single ring lay on the desk beside her. They were never far from her side, and Corinne knew the old woman slept with the keys under her pillow. One key was to her journal while the other was to a large iron-bound chest that was never moved from beneath her high bed, not even to disturb the dust that collected there. Why she bothered locking those two items when she never left the room Corinne did not know. She forced a smile to her lips as she poured the wine into the glass.

"A fine day, Corinne."

"Yes, madame."

"I thought I heard something a little while ago . . . the sound of distant pistol shots. Has there been more trouble with the farmers?"

"I don't know. I didn't hear anything," Corinne lied. "If madame eats too many petits fours, she will not eat her lunch," she added, eyeing the delicately iced cakes.

"Do have one yourself, my dear," the comtess said, smiling a rather sad smile. "There is no need to protect me from bad news, Corinne. Your friend Captain Winslow has told me of the situation with the peasants."

Corinne nibbled a cake, frowning. "I should not have brought him to you."

"On the contrary, I shall always be grateful that you did. He brought me news that made all my lonely years of exile worthwhile."

"That you have a granddaughter," Corinne said, her feelings on the subject transparent as her lips went down in a sullen pout. As the comtess's only attendant, Corinne had hoped for a considerable bequest when the old lady died, which, judging by her failing strength, could be at any time. The existence of a granddaughter clouded that hope.

The comtess sipped her wine and gazed out of her window at the formal gardens below. The chateau was a gothic structure with dramatically thrusting slender stone towers that used the minimum amount of stone to support the maximum amount of glass-enclosed space. Approaching the chateau for the first time as a young bride, the comtess had thought the beautiful old building almost too fragile and ethereal to be real—a fairy castle painted in watercolors on an amethyst sky. The gardens were laid out in sculptured and geometric patterns that made English gardens seem rather carelessly natural by comparison. For a moment she looked at the serenity of the picture framed by her window and ached for the lost years, for the dashing young Frenchman who had been gone for so long now.

"Madame," Corinne said. "I was remarking that Captain Winslow brought you news that you have a granddaughter."

"Yes, indeed," the comtess answered softly. "Our line is not yet extinct." She tapped the surface of her desk with her delicate white fingers, considering again all of the implications of the story Stede Winslow had told her.

"Sir Laurence Tregarth hid her away in a school in England. All those years I thought my Regine's marriage had been childless, but he had her tucked away. He is a wicked man, Corinne. I cannot understand why Regine married him in her maturity when she could not abide him in her youth." She glanced in the direction of her bed, hidden behind deep burgundy draperies. Her fingers drifted to the keys on the desk, fingering them thoughtfully. "I do hope Captain Winslow will arrive today. Otherwise, I fear it will be too late. Perhaps he was unable to keep his promise to return. Corinne—"

"Yes, madame?" Corinne was suddenly alert, feeling the urgency in the old woman's tone.

"If the good captain does not arrive today, I must entrust you with a mission of great importance. Oh, how I wish I had given him the chest when he first came to see me! I was so stunned, you see, and not thinking clearly."

"The chest, madame," Corinne prompted, her black eyes gleaming with anticipation.

"Under my bed. This is the key. The chest contains all of the D'Arcy family jewels. I had them all placed in velvet-lined trays when I knew I would never wear them again. They will all belong to my granddaughter now. I was going to ask Captain Winslow to deliver them to her. I believe I can trust him. His father was my brother's son, you know. Stede is, I suppose, my great-nephew. But even if he were not a Winslow, there is something about him, don't you think? Beneath that rather reckless and impudent manner there is a noble and courageous spirit. Didn't you feel it, Corinne?"

"Oh, yes, madame, indeed I did," Corinne breathed fervently, her limbs turning to water at the thought of the feelings she had for Stede Winslow.

"If anything happens to me . . . will you see that he gets the chest? Ask him to deliver it to Darcy. I made a new will, leaving the chateau and everything I own to her, but if what Captain Winslow tells me is going to happen comes to pass, then only the contents of the chest will have any value. I am quite sure my granddaughter will see to your welfare, Corinne. And you may choose one of the pieces for yourself."

One of the pieces, Corinne thought resentfully. During all the years when she had waited on the old crow, where was the precious granddaughter then? Draw my bath, Corinne, fetch my wine. Corinne, my feet are cold.

"Why, of course, I'll see that the chest goes to its rightful owner," Corinne said sweetly. "Do you think you should give me the key now?"

The comtess smiled. "All in good time. Perhaps I'll take a little nap before lunch. I feel so dreadfully tired today."

While she slept, Corinne sat in the kitchen gossiping with the other maids and flirting with the footmen. All of the talk below stairs was of the outbreaks of violence that moved ever nearer to the chateau.

Just after noon, a lathered horse came streaking through the formal gardens, hooves heedless of delicate flowers and crushable grasses. The rider lay low against the neck of the horse, knees urging the animal at breakneck speed toward the chateau.

Corinne and the other servants rushed outside in response to a loud hail from the approaching rider. Corinne recognized Stede's voice at once, and her face broke into a joyful smile as he swung down from his mount and tossed the reins to the nearest footman.

"Quickly—you must barricade all the doors and windows on the ground floor. There is a mob hard on my heels, and I fear they are coming straight to the chateau. Corinne—go to the comtess immediately and pack a few things for her. You men, what are you waiting for? Barricades—anything to slow the progress of those bloodthirsty devils coming this way. One of you women go and tell the stablemaster to make a carriage and the fastest team of horses ready for a journey. The carriage is to be waiting at the tradesmen's entrance in five minutes."

"Stede—" Corinne plucked at his arm, her eyes wide with fright. "Will they attack all of us . . . even we who are not *aristos?*"

Before he could answer they heard the sound—a distant rumbling growl of angry voices coming over the hilltop. It was the fearsome sound of collective hate, the roar of men spoiling for blood.

"Go to your mistress. I will be there in a moment." Stede gave her a slight push. She sped away.

Stede remained long enough to be sure that the entrance doors were barricaded with the heaviest furniture and sent the male servants to do the same to the massive windows. They worked with one eye on Stede and the other on the small army marching down the hillside like an angry column of ants. The moment he left to go to the comtess, the servants dropped everything and ran. The life of a woman most of them had never seen was not worth the sacrifice of their own.

Bursting into the comtess's chambers, Stede bowed respectfully. "Forgive the abruptness of my arrival. I trust we can hold a proper conversation en route to my ship." His eyes swept the room. There was a single iron–bound chest standing in the middle of the floor and on top of it a leather bound book. There was no sign of luggage, and the comtess, standing next to the chest, was obviously not dressed for travel.

"Please, madame, you must come with me immediately," Stede said, moving to her side. He picked up her hand, and her fingers lay limply across his palm. She was deathly pale but looked at him wtih a steady gaze and a sad smile.

"I cannot leave my home, Captain Winslow. To do so would be to give it into the hands of undisciplined peasants who might damage priceless treasures. But you must take Corinne and this chest, which contains family heirlooms I wish you to deliver to my granddaughter, Darcy."

"Stede, we must leave now," Corrine said, jumping from one foot to the other in her haste to be gone. She had donned a long hooded cloak and held a portmanteau so hastily packed that pieces of clothing were visible from the opening.

"And how shall you defend the chateau?" Stede asked the comtess gently. "I'm afraid that your servants are fleeing at this moment. Please, you must come with me now. You have a brave and gallant heart, but alas, no means of defense against the blind fury of a mob."

"I will not leave," the comtess repeated, her eyes bright in her pale and shrunken face. She looked like a Dresden figurine about to crumble from sheer age.

"Corinne, get the comtess's cloak," Stede instructed. He stepped forward and picked up the old lady. She closed her eyes tightly but did not resist.

"Stede—wait," Corinne screamed as he shouldered open the

door. "The chest—we must take the chest. It is too heavy for me to carry alone."

He glanced back. The howl of the mob rose from the court-yard below. There were angry shouts as they crowded about the entrance to the chateau carrying pikes and sabres. Some picked up rocks and hurled them against the walls. There was the sound of shattering glass.

"Empty the chest," Stede said. "Put the contents into a reticule—anything that you will be able to carry. I will take the comtess to the carriage and come back for you." He disappeared through the door.

Sobbing with fright, Corinne bent to unlock the chest. The key trembled in her hands as she tried to turn the ancient lock. Nothing happened. She jiggled the key frantically, unthinkingly knocking the book to the floor, as another crash from the courtyard below made her heart skid.

The chest had not been opened for so long . . . perhaps it would not open? The more she tugged and twisted, the less inclined the key was to release the mechanism. After a few minutes, she gave up and attempted dragging the heavy chest across the floor. She had dragged it as far as the door when Stede returned. "It wouldn't open," she wailed.

"Go to your mistress. I'll bring it," he said.

Corinne hesitated. There was a roar from below followed by a great splintering crash that could only mean a battering ram had breached the barricade at the front doors. She turned and fled, forgetting to give Stede the key in her haste.

Stede eyed the chest. The weight of the iron-bound box alone would slow down the horses. He pulled a pistol from his belt and fired at the lock. The sound of the exploding pistol would undoubtedly guide the mob to these chambers, he thought as he bent to raise the lid of the chest. He hoped the contents were worth the risk.

A moment later he looked down on an array of jewels that would surely ransom an emperor. Some of the precious stones were set in gold and silver necklaces and bracelets or fine old brooches while others merely lay on their black velvet bed looking like brilliant fragments of stained glass against the night sky. Beneath the tray, carefully wrapped in chamois leather, were gold goblets encrusted with gems, placques, amulets, and several pouches containing smaller pieces of jewelry and rings.

Dumping Corinne's clothes on the floor, Stede quickly scooped the jewels into the portmanteau. As he emerged from the comtess's chambers, the first wild-eyed men appeared at the foot of the stairs. Behind them, their comrades were already rampaging through the rooms of the chateau, plundering and vandalizing.

"There's one of them!" a red-faced farmer shouted. "Kill him! Kill him!" the others chorused, jostling each other to be the first up the staircase. "Where is the old woman? Where is the comtess?" someone in the rear shouted.

Stede reloaded his pistol, the portmanteau at his feet. He aimed it at the chest of the nearest man. "Stand where you are or you're a dead man." His voice was quiet, contrasting sharply with the shrieks below but compelling attention. The man hesitated. A second later his companions forced him forward and Stede fired. As the body of the man fell back, drenching those nearest him in blood, Stede ran back into the comtess's chambers, slamming shut the door.

The window was high above the courtyard still filled with a milling crowd of peasants trying to get into the chateau. Stede pushed open the window and climbed on to the narrow ledge outside. There was pounding on the door behind him.

Tucking the portmanteau under his arm, he inched along the ledge to the corner of the building. None of the men below looked up. The ledge came to an end and he was forced to find precarious footholds between the stones of the wall, clinging to window ledges for support as he descended toward a stout tree growing close to the tradesmen's entrance.

Stede was sure-footed in the rigging of a ship, and he used every trick of balance he had ever learned. The portmanteau was an almost deadly encumbrance, and more than once he considered discarding it, but the memory of the fortune inside and the anticipation of spilling those jewels into the lap of the delectable Darcy Sinclair stayed his hand.

At last his hand grasped the branch of the tree, and he swung down into the waiting carriage as Corinne took the whip to the horses. The comtess lay simply across the seat and Stede assumed she had fainted. Above them the window burst into glittering shards of glass as the peasants vented their rage at the escaping carriage.

Stede jerked the reins from Corinne's hands as the horses bolted in fright. "See to the comtess," he shouted, giving the horses their heads.

"She's dead," Corinne screamed back at him. "Shall I push her out of the carriage?"

"If you do I'll fling you after her," Stede yelled. They rounded the corner, and the mob in the courtyard heard the sound of the carriage and horses and raced to intercept it.

The whip in Corinne's hand lashed at the men who plucked at the carriage and Stede's boot went into the chest of a man who dived for the reins. There had been no time to reload the pistol in his belt.

For a second the carriage swayed alarmingly but broke away from the men trying to slow the panicked horses. Then they were free and galloping toward the hills. Stede glanced down at the old woman. He had removed her body from the danger of the chateau, but from the small smile playing about her pallid lips her spirit had been left behind in the home of the husband she had loved and who had loved her so much that he had given her a collection of jewels that rivaled those of the king himself.

Chapter Eight

GWYNETH WAS A quick and apt pupil. So long confined to her silent world and ignored by the other servants, she eagerly mastered the art of communicating with Darcy.

Darcy learned to her astonishment that Gwyneth had already picked up the rudimentary elements of lip reading from years of studying the movement of the mouths of those around her. As a child learns to speak by imitating sounds, Gwyneth had learned to interpret some of what was being said by watching lip movements and matching them to subsequent actions. Now Darcy concentrated on teaching Gwyneth to move her own lips while Darcy strove to understand what she was 'saying'.

Sir Laurence Tregarth had stormed out of the house to lead a party of men in search of Stede. Cullen accompanied his father, and they did not return for several days. Darcy and Gwyneth worked feverishly to master the art of 'speaking' to one another during the short respite, and Darcy conveyed her plan to run away from the enforced marriage to Sir Laurence.

"Gwyneth, I don't know how we shall live," Darcy enunciated the words carefully but soundlessly. "I have no money. But I want you to come with me. There must be some way we can make a living. I was quite good with both French and Latin at school and especially fond of arithmetic. Perhaps I could find a position as a governess."

Gwyneth smiled happily and nodded her head, mouthing "When shall we go?" Her mistress did not know how eager she was to leave since the day Master Cullen had come upon her unexpectedly and remarked insinuatingly that the little mute was growing into a lovely woman. Gwyneth had seen some of the younger scullery maids brought back to their quarters sobbing and bruised after visits to the chambers of Sir Laurence and his son.

Darcy sat at her dressing table, reluctant to go down to dinner for fear Sir Laurence had returned. Gwyneth was airing the dress Darcy would wear, shaking it in front of the fire and brushing the velvet with a small soft-bristled brush.

"Getting out of the house will be our most difficult task," Darcy said. "The bridge to the mainland is guarded by the watchtower, and there is always a man or two passing by the windows. Sir Laurence has acted as though we were under seige since Stede Winslow managed to get into the house. I wonder how he did get in without crossing the bridge?"

Gwyneth watched her lips, then placed the blue velvet dress down on the bed and went to the desk. Dipping a quill into the inkwell, she drew a diagram with rapid strokes.

Darcy studied the drawing. There was no mistaking the object Gwyneth had drawn in one of the three boxes she had made on the paper.

"This is the dungeon," Darcy said, pointing to the box with the rack. "Here are the stone steps. The next box represents the wine cellar . . . but, what's this? There are three sections to the cellars—not two? Is that what you are telling me? Gwyneth, come, you must show me."

Dusk was creeping along the chill passageways of Tregarth Hall as the two young women descended to the chambers built into the rock of the bluff. Gwyneth carried an oil lantern, and Darcy stayed close behind her. They placed slippered feet carefully on the worn steps, hands trailing the dripping stone walls to be sure they did not stray too close to the unprotected edge of the steps.

They averted their eyes as they hurried past the dungeon, along the dank passage that led to the wine cellar. Rats darted out of their path, some turning tiny malevolent eyes toward the intruders and shrieking defiance. Past the cobweb–hung racks of wine bottles, the lantern flickering bravely in the gloom, they came at last to an iron-studded door. It was almost rotted with age, hidden behind a stone buttress.

Darcy lifted the latch and pushed the door. It creaked open to reveal a third chamber and beyond, a narrow passage. Darcy was about to enter the passage when Gwyneth caught her arm, shaking her head.

"But where does it lead? I must know," Darcy mouthed the words, unsure if Gwyneth could read her lips in the dim light.

Placing the lantern carefully on the floor, Gwyneth moved her hands rhythmically, her lips trying to form a word to match her gestures. She then pointed down the dark passage.

"Gwyneth, I don't understand you. Wait here, and I'll go and have a look." Picking up the lantern, Darcy entered the passage.

She shivered in an icy dampness that closed in upon her like a smothering cloak. There was a sound like a distant whispering breath that was both familiar and ghostly. Echoes, she thought, every sound has a distorted echo down the stone passageways.

All at once she came upon another flight of stone steps. As she was about to step down on to the first, Gwyneth clutched at her, pulling her back. Darcy stopped abruptly, waving the lantern to illuminate what lay beyond. All but three of the steps were submerged in churning black water. Darcy drew back, smelling the tang of brine and fish.

"The sea," she breathed. "You were trying to tell me the sea gets in here." She was disappointed. This was not another way out of the castle as she had assumed. Then she looked at Gwyneth again, realizing that the girl was again making waves with her hands, mouthing the word . . . what word?

"High tide!" Darcy said excitedly. "You're telling me the sea only comes in at high tide. Can we get out at low tide?"

Gwyneth pointed back toward the way they had come.

"Very well, you're right. We shall be missed if we don't hurry. You can tell me upstairs."

Before Darcy went down to dinner, she had determined from Gwyneth that at low tide the steps led to a cave that in turn opened to a tiny pebble beach. The cave and steps were inundated at high tide, but at low tide the men of the household often used the beach to launch a boat for fishing expeditions in the bountiful waters lapping at the ramparts of the cliff. The boat, Darcy learned, was moored in the cave, tied to a stake to allow it to float up with the incoming tide.

Darcy went down to dinner, her head full of plans. They would need warm clothes. She would have to sell her mother's jewelry in order to buy passage on the coach. She considered asking Cullen for help and discarded the idea. If they could reach London there were friends who would help. Her fellow students from the Grafton School would surely know of a family seeking a governess and a lady's maid.

Preoccupied with her plans, Darcy walked into the dining room to find Sir Laurence seated at the head of the table. He was alone.

"Your smuggler made good his escape," he snapped, draining a glass of wine and motioning for a footman to refill it. "We searched every cove and inlet that could hide his ship. He has no doubt gone skulking back to France. But he'll be back. He won't be able to resist a large order for wines and spirits from the Inn of the Blue Lantern."

He drank another glass of wine while Darcy was taking her place at the opposite end of the table. "Cullen isn't back?" she inquired.

Sir Laurence regarded her with hooded eyes. "He went to visit his bride-to-be. We are alone. You look quite lovely tonight, my dear, although those somber velvet dresses you wear do little to enhance your beauty. Why do you not wear the evening gowns I had made for you?"

"Silk and gauze are flimsy for the icy drafts of Tregarth Hall," Darcy responded. "The fires warm the rooms, but one does have to move about cold corridors, too."

He regarded her over the rim of his wine glass. "No matter,

the lily needs little gilding. The candlelight paints rose-colored lights on your fair complexion and weaves tawny shadows into your hair.''

Darcy was startled at his choice of words. She looked up to search his face to see if it had been deliberate. He stared back at her with a mask-like lack of expression, concentrating on his wine.

Tawny Rose. Darcy had been very young when her mother went away with Sir Laurence Tregarth. *My little tawny rose . . . oh, my darling, how can I bear to leave you? But it's just for a little while; then we'll be together again. Why do I call you my tawny rose? Because you have my coloring, dear. Did you know that once a famous artist painted a portrait of me and it was called Tawny Rose? The picture, you see, was commissioned by a man who loved me, and that was the name he gave to me.*

Because it was the last time she ever saw her mother, Darcy had never forgotten the conversation.

"A penny for your thoughts," Sir Laurence said, his voice slurring slightly with the wine. Darcy wished the footman would hurry with the soup tureen.

"I was wondering how my mother really died," she said quietly. "And how a man could be so cold-blooded as to send word of his wife's death while she was still alive."

"I see. The smuggler Winslow told you some far-fetched stories and you believe him." Sir Laurence rose unsteadily to his feet and stumbled down the length of the table toward her. She did not move but tilted her chin and stared at him. "I don't understand why you found it necessary to kill my mother. She was a beautiful, exciting woman. You could have had her as well as the D'Arcy wealth."

Sir Laurence spoke without thinking. "Because she was pining after another man, and I could not tolerate it." He broke off, realizing what the wine was doing to his tongue. "Why you little doxie, you cause my tongue to run away with me. That is not what I meant. Your mother died of yellow fever. But had she lived I might well have been driven to kill her

77

because she lay in my arms and imagined me to be another man."

Reaching her side, he leaned on the back of her chair, looking down at her. "When I sent word to the Chateau D'Arcy that she was dead I knew that she would probably die before the ship reached France. I needed funds and thought perhaps the comtess would send money to have her daughter's body returned for burial. But none were forthcoming."

He paused, his eyes drifting down the bodice of her dress. "My thoughts have returned repeatedly to you, my dear, these past few days." His finger traced the line of her cheek, followed the curve of her chin, down her throat, lingering near the soft swelling of her breast.

"It is not me you want," she said, "but my mother. You are extracting some sort of twisted revenge on a dead woman because she did not love you."

"Perhaps. But you see, Darcy, there is also your grandmother's failing health and the fact that you, sweet child, could become an heiress at any moment . . . making you twice as attractive as your mother." His hand closed possessively on her shoulder.

Her hand clasped the handle of the knife lying beside her plate. "Take your hand off me," she said coldly. "You are not my husband yet."

He threw back his head and laughed. "Very good, my dear. I wouldn't have it any other way."

At that moment, the footmen appeared, carrying a soup tureen and basket of crusty bread. But as the meal progressed, Darcy watched Sir Laurence drink more wine and squirmed under the assault of his eyes. She worried about going to her chambers alone when dinner was over.

The hall was dark and still, the last of the servants had retired for the night, and the fire in the hearth glowed feebly beneath a white mountain of ash. Sir Laurence dropped the empty bottle to the floor beside his chair and rose.

He walked purposefully toward the staircase, his footsteps sure. Other men drank themselves into oblivion, but Sir Laurence held his spirits well. At the top of the stairs he paused, looking toward Darcy's chambers. Not yet, my sweet, he thought. First I remove my boots, and then I come upon you silently. He went to his own room, pushed open the door, and stopped abruptly.

Lady Evadne was standing beside his bed. A candle flickered in the wall sconce near her, casting red shadows on the white cape she wore. She smiled at him, letting the cape fall to the floor. Except for two ribbons, one tied prettily about her neck and the second encircling one white thigh, she wore nothing.

Sir Laurence kicked the door shut behind him and peeled the cutaway coat from his shoulders, allowing it to fall to the floor. "I thought you were entertaining my son tonight."

Evadne pouted prettily. "I've been waiting up here for ages. Your son cannot hold his brandy. He's long asleep. Father had two of the grooms carry him to a guest room, and I slipped away to visit you."

Sir Laurence began to unbutton his ruffled shirt. Evadne breathed heavily with excitement, and her pale eyes glittered, the pupils large black circles that gave her an almost occult air of sensual depravity. Her arms went around his neck, pulling him to her mouth impatiently. Her flesh was warm. Too warm for the cold room.

He pulled away with sudden awareness, looking at the languid eyelids, the crushed coiffure. "You have been with Cullen. You have come to me from his bed. How dare you lie with that whelp and then come crawling to me for your satisfaction?" He held her by the throat in a vicious grip.

"Laurence . . . " she whimpered, licking her lips. "You're the one who wanted me to marry him. You know it was you I wanted, never him. Laurence, please, don't be cruel tonight . . . just love me."

For answer, he thrust her from him. "Your father would have cut you off without a penny if I had married you. He is well aware of my gambling losses and has heard too many exaggerated stories of my little diversions. Cullen, on the other hand, is young enough to have his peccadillos excused and can be considered most eligible. Doesn't every young woman in London pant after him, including my fair bride-to-be? No, Cullen is a wise choice. Keeps you in the family, so to speak.''

"But I need you so. . . ." she whispered, twining her arms around him, confident that he would not remain so aloof.

"You offer no challenge anymore, Evadne. I weary of your pursuit." But his actions belied his words.

Chapter Nine

AT THE INN of the Blue Lantern, Philippe paced slowly back and forth in front of the fire in the public saloon, his cane clicking on the floor.

"Why don't you sit down and have a glass of ale?" Violet suggested, tired of his pacing. "Ain't nothing you can do." Her eyes darted nervously toward the corner of the room where the disguised Excise men waited.

"How can we warn him?" Philippe repeated under his breath. "There must be a way. A beacon fire, perhaps, on the cliff?"

Violet polished tankards and said impatiently, "I told you, they've got men all over everywhere. You'd never get a fire started on the cliff—they're patrolling up there every few minutes. Besides, you don't know when he'll get here. Would you keep a fire burning night after night? What if he comes in the daylight? Stede Winslow has been reckless enough to do that."

"Keep your voice down; they will hear," Philippe warned. "I am going to walk along the cliff. There must be some way to warn Stede that the King's men are lying in wait for him." Philippe picked up the Garrick coat lying over the back of a chair and wrapped it about his frail body. The Excise men barely glanced at him as he limped out into the night.

A pale crescent moon hung in a cloudless sky, and pinpoints of starlight were echoed in the phosphorescent cresting of gentle waves breaking in the rocky cove below the cliff where Philippe had watched for the return of Stede's schooner for three nights. Why had the Excise men appeared in force tonight, Philippe wondered again.

"Who goes there?" a gruff voice demanded suddenly.

Philippe stopped. A shadowy figure loomed in his path.

"I have been lodging at the inn," Philippe said. "I wanted to take a walk on such a fine night."

"Ah, a Frenchie," the voice said. "Well, the good weather won't last; there'll be a change with the tide. I can smell it." He paused, and Philippe felt the man's eyes scrutinize him, coming back to rest on the cane that supported his weight. "A bit safer here for a Frenchie than in your precious Paree, isn't it now? I hear the mobs are destroying the city. No law and order there, hey? Well, you'd best get on back to the inn because the King's men are expecting a ship to put into that cove tonight and there could be trouble."

Philippe turned and retraced his footsteps. Tonight. How could they be so sure? He had waited for Stede for three nights. Perhaps they had received a signal that the ship was coming? Or did they assume that he might slip into the cove under cover of the bad weather the man said was imminent? Or perhaps someone knew exactly when Stede would arrive and had informed them?

He thought suddenly of Violet, the barmaid at the inn. She has been particularly jumpy all evening, continually watching the door that led down to the fish cellar where the smugglers usually entered with their contraband. In contrast to her usual lethargic approach to her duties, tonight she had polished tankards, refueled the fire repeatedly, cleaned counter and tables.

And how did the Excise man know exactly which of the many coves Stede would slip his schooner into? The night Philippe sailed with him into that particular cove Stede had said, "Our ship is hidden by the headland all the way in. There are dangerous offshore rocks with only a narrow channel to shore. Even the small fishing boats avoid that cove. We have to carry our kegs of wine a little further, but the safety of the anchorage justifies the extra labor.''

Violet, Philippe thought. She has to be the informer. Her father would know when a consignment of French wines was expected because he would have to clear space to stow the cargo and have payment ready. Philippe quickened his pace, wincing as pain shot up his leg from his mutilated foot. He was remembering that one of the Excise men appeared to be on excessively familiar terms with Violet when she served their evening meal.

The Inn of the Blue Lantern was built on its own sheltered cove, with cellars in the cliffs as was the custom in this part of Cornwall. Tied up in the cove were half a dozen fishing boats belonging to the innkeeper, Albert, and his family. The boats provided fresh fish for the inn's patrons. Around the headland and into another inlet was Stede's safe anchorage.

Returning to the inn, Philippe avoided the public saloon and went directly to his room. A few minutes later he made his way outside again, carrying under his caped overcoat the lantern from his room and an extra supply of oil.

The Excise men were watching Stede's cove and there was no one in sight when Philippe approached Albert's fishing boats, tied up in the inn's cove. A short time later, three of the boats burst into flame, sending orange plumes soaring over the cliff and visible for miles out to sea.

Stede took the spyglass from his eye. ''Bring her about,'' he ordered. ''That's a warning beacon if I ever saw one.'' He added under his breath, ''Bless you, Philippe.''

''What course, sir?'' the helmsman called over the creaking rigging and slap of gentle swells against the hull. There was little wind, and the canvas hung limply.

''We'll heave to until dawn. There's a fog hatching; I feel it in the air. We'll slip in under cover of the mists.''

Stede went below to his cabin, where Corinne was curled up on the bunk. She looked at him with acute misery in her sloe black eyes. Her normally pink cheeks were a delicate green. She moaned and pulled a blanket over her head.

"You'd feel better if you'd put on a warm wrap and go on deck," Stede said.

Corinne turned her face to the bulkhead.

"Suit yourself," Stede said. "But I'm afraid we can't go in tonight. You'll have to put up with the rocking of the ship until dawn."

"Go away and let me die," Corinne said from the depths of her blanket.

Stede patted her rump reassuringly and went to the galley for supper. His first officer, a brawny North countryman named Chalmers with a surprisingly soft voice, was finishing his supper. "Weather coming," he remarked. He was given to monosyllables and fragments of sentences, but a *sotto voce* curse on his lips had the power to make crewmen shake in their boots.

Stede nodded. "Fog. We'll use it as cover in the morning. Better get some sleep, Mr. Chalmers."

"Aye, sir." He rose, bending massive shoulders so that his head would not hit the bulkhead.

Waiting for the ship's cook to bring his meal, Stede wondered for the hundredth time what he would do with Corinne when they reached the Inn of the Blue Lantern. During the mad dash from the chateau to the sea that had seemed the least of his problems. Several times they had detoured around peasant mobs. They had taken little–used lanes and had avoided villages and farms.

On the second evening, as dusk fell, Stede had buried the body of the comtess beneath a sheltering tree, silently promising that when the terror ended he would return to place her remains in consecrated ground. Corinne had crossed herself and whimpered that they should keep moving.

He had not intended to bring Corinne aboard his ship. If he had, the portrait of the Tawny Rose would not have been hanging in his cabin. He had barely been able to prevent

Corinne from slashing it with the knife she snatched from his belt.

"That is the name you murmur in your sleep!" Corinne had shrieked. "That is what you call your ship. And all the time you tell me it is me that you love."

He held her, dodging the deadly blade of the knife. "Are you jealous of a ghost? She is dead these many years. That is the daughter of the comtess—the one who ran away with my father. But he did not live to marry her."

"Then why do you keep her picture here in your cabin? Why did you not give it to the comtess? Why do you call your ship *Tawny Rose?*" Corinne demanded.

Why, indeed, Stede thought.

He had removed the portrait from his cabin, entrusting its care to his taciturn first officer, Chalmers, and the *Tawny Rose* slipped out into the English Channel where the motion of the vessel quickly incapacitated Corinne.

Sitting in the galley with a savory plate of stew in front of him and a long loaf of French bread to help it down, Stede's blood quickened as he thought of the daughter of the Tawny Rose. So like her mother she might have stepped down from the portrait. It had been difficult, that first night he met Darcy, to keep from sweeping her into his arms. He felt as if he had been waiting for her all his life. What a blow it had been when she uttered the hated name of Tregarth as her protector.

Stede had studied the portrait that night, noting the similarities and the differences. If the artist had captured the likeness accurately, then the lovely woman of the portrait was more aware of her allure, more flirtatious than Darcy Sinclair. Darcy's eyes were fearlessly honest, with no hint of coquetry. She would never play games with a man, pretending emotions she did not feel. She was the portrait of the Tawny Rose brought to life with all of the flaws removed.

Reposing under his bunk, where Corinne now battled her *mal de mer*, was the portmanteau that would free Darcy forever from the house of Tregarth. Stede smiled and bit into a hunk of bread, wishing it were dawn so that he could take Darcy her inheritance.

Darcy lay in her bed, wide awake and sorry she had not asked Gwyneth to spend the night in her room. But that might have aroused suspicion.

The house creaked and groaned as ancient timbers warped and stretched. Outside, the sea murmured restlessly. Each sound sent Darcy's eyes to her door. She had dropped the long wooden bolt of the lock and placed two chairs in front of the door.

Once she thought she heard Sir Laurence's footsteps outside, but he had gone in the other direction. An hour had passed. He must be asleep by now.

Several times she had begun to doze, but the image of Sir Laurence's face brought her fearfully back to wakefulness. She saw the hooded eyes, the cruel lips, the way his roving gaze had undressed her body throughout dinner.

At last, unable to bear the tension any longer, Darcy climbed out of bed. Several hours had elapsed since Gwyneth showed her the passage that led from the cellar to the sea. By now the tide had surely receded.

Dressing hurriedly, Darcy threw some of her clothes into a valise, wrapped her mother's jewel case in her petticoats and placed it in the center of the bag. The traveling dress she put on was adorned with a strange-looking ribbon rosette at the waist that concealed Stede's silver buckle, dropped the night he visited Tregarth Hall. She had sewn it to her dress and covered it with ribbon for fear Sir Laurence would recognize the crest.

Removing her barricade, she opened the bedroom door a crack and peered out. The landing appeared to be deserted. Creeping past Sir Laurence's door, she was startled to hear a woman's voice. Evadne! Darcy breathed a sigh of relief. Sir Laurence was not likely to come looking for her this night.

Gwyneth was awake, sitting beside a tiny bundle of her

possessions in the room she shared with two other maids, both of whom were deep in exhausted sleep. Darcy beckoned for Gwyneth to follow, and they made their way down the stairs and through the hall, darting through pools of moonlight, along empty corridors, past closed doors, until they reached the stone steps leading to the cellars.

"Careful!" Darcy cautioned aloud, forgetting Gwyneth could not hear. "The steps are so slimy tonight."

"That they are, my dear Darcy." Cullen's voice came from the bottom of the stairs.

"Cullen!" Darcy cried, straining to see him in the faint light cast by the lantern Gwyneth carried. "What are you doing down there in the dark?"

He came up the steps toward them, a bottle of wine in his hand. "Looking for a nightcap. My lantern burned out. More to the point, my sweet, what are you and your maid doing down here at this time of night? Aha! Valise and traveling bundle. Why, you naughty thing . . . you were running away." From his uncertain step and the tone of his voice, he had already had several nightcaps.

"Cullen, please, come with us," Darcy said impulsively. "We are going to take a boat and cross to the other side of the cove, then make our way to the inn and catch the coach for London in the morning. Cullen, you can't marry Lady Evadne— she's in your father's bed at this very moment."

He stretched his arm across the steps to the wall, blocking their progress. "And what, pray tell, would we live on? Evadne brings a large dowry with her, and I'm well aware that she prefers my father to me. Good lord, Darcy, you're such an innocent. Don't you see, if you marry Father and I marry Evadne, it will be perfect. They can go to each other's chambers and so can we. What does it matter who is married to whom . . . or is that whom to who?" He laughed drunkenly, his hand slipping down the wall slightly. "Must be careful, these steps are slippery as grease. Come on, Darcy, let's move to a safer spot to discuss this."

"Cullen, I can't marry your father. The thought of him touching me makes my skin crawl." Darcy looked at her first love sadly, realizing that the prospect of Cullen making love to her was equally repulsive. What had happened to that breathless longing she had once felt, she wondered. Her schoolgirl crush on the only male to visit her in the smotheringly female confines of the Grafton School had somehow all been swept away in one heart-stopping moment that night she had stepped into the Inn of the Blue Lantern and met Stede.

"Nevertheless, old girl," Cullen was saying, "I can't let you run away. Too dangerous by far. Besides, Father would kill me. You too, probably." He seized Darcy's arm in one hand and Gwyneth's in the other. In trying to push them back from the steps, his feet went out from under him. If he had not been holding on to them, he would have gone over the edge of the steps and fallen to the stone floor below.

"Damn," he muttered, scrambling to regain his balance. "Father has got to put a rail down that blasted flight of stairs." He was dragging them back along the corridor.

Darcy struggled but could not dislodge him. At the end of the corridor was a bell pull, and when they reached it Cullen tugged on it, summoning servants.

Pulling her arm free, Darcy cried, "Gwyneth—run!" But it was hopeless; servants were appearing everywhere. They were quickly surrounded. Darcy wanted to weep with frustration.

"Stand aside," an imperious voice demanded. "Let me through." Darcy's heart sank as the servants fell back to admit Sir Laurence.

"What is this?" he asked.

"They were running away, Father," Cullen said with a slight smirk. "I caught them and brought them back. I say, Father, that alarm bell you rigged up must have awakened the entire household."

Sir Laurence stepped closer to Darcy, and for an instant she thought he would strike her. Instead, he said in a cold flat voice, "Take the mute back to her quarters. I've no doubt she has no real conception of what my wily bride-to-be planned."

As Gwyneth was ushered away by two footmen, Darcy looked into Sir Laurence's face and felt a surge of fear. "What about me? What are you going to do?"

Sir Laurence turned to his personal valet. "Take her down to the dungeon. We must teach her a lesson. You will not attempt foolishness such as this again, Darcy. A few hours down there will allow you to see the folly of your ways."

Darcy could not stop shivering as she was propelled down the steps.

Chapter Ten

DARCY PRAYED FOR deliverance in the complete darkness of the narrow cell. At first she had paced nervously back and forth, but as time passed she had grown very tired and was now sitting in a corner, her forehead resting against the damp stone wall, her legs curled under her. A large rat scurried by, and Darcy pulled the skirts of her travelling dress more closely around her. How long had she been here? Five minutes? An hour? Two hours?

She had pinched her nostrils together to ward off the rank odor that seemed at that moment like the breath of medieval ghosts. How many had died here dreadfully at the hands of past Tregarths she wondered numbly.

Then she heard footsteps on the stairs and recognized them as Sir Laurence's. As the key turned in the lock, she stood up and hugged herself, terrified. The light from his flickering candle was blinding at first, and it was several moments before she was able to see his gaunt silhouette looming ominously in the doorway. Reflected flames danced in his eyes.

"You stupid child," he said coldly. "Don't you realize the waters surrounding Tregarth Hall are dangerous even for an experienced boatman? You would have perished out there in a small boat. You would not have been strong enough to row against the current." As he spoke, he walked slowly toward her. She stepped backward until she was pressed against the wall. Then he placed his candle on the floor.

A moment later, Sir Laurence fingered her hair, which had come loose and tumbled over her shoulder. "Your hair is exactly the same color as your mother's . . . like a lion's mane, all tawny shadows.''

There was that word again. Darcy looked him directly in the eye. "Why do you force me into marriage? What manner of man wants a woman who does not want him?''

"Women don't know what they want," he said, his fingers tightening in her hair until she bit back a cry of pain. "That's why the law makes you our chattels. So that we can make these decisions for you. Protect you from your own foolishness.''

"And control any assets we might have," Darcy said, thinking of what Stede had told her about her grandmother's wealth.

"Your assets, my dear, are clearly evident," Sir Laurence's breath was like a cold wind against her neck. He was standing very close to her, pressing her to the wall.

She screamed. The sound reverberated about the stone walls. Twisting to one side, she pushed him away and made a dash for the door. He was too quick for her, and within moments he had pinned her arms against the wall. Darcy was sobbing now.

His breathing was growing more uneven. He cursed as she again twisted to elude him. Now his hands grasped her waist, and he held her so that she could not move. He was chuckling deep in his throat.

There was a sudden, sickening thud of something heavy striking flesh, and the chuckling ended in a gasp. Sir Laurence slid to the floor behind her, hands slipping down her body as he fell. The rosette and silver buckle came loose and were gripped in his hand as he crashed to the floor.

Darcy opened her eyes to look into the reassuring face of Gwyneth, who lost no time in bending over Sir Laurence's inert form. Shaking with fear, Darcy watched, certain that he would leap up and overpower them both.

They looked down at Sir Laurence. There was a trickle of blood on the stone floor next to the iron mask Gwyneth had used to render him unconscious. Pausing only long enough to snatch up the candle, they ran. They slowed down only to descend the slippery steps leading to the cave. A gust of cold air swept in from the sea, blowing out the candle, and they held each other's hands as they splashed into ankle-deep water, feeling sharply pointed rocks under their feet.

At length, they stood on a tiny crescent beach, the sea lapping at pebbles and crushed shells. The moon sailed out from behind the cliff, illuminating the boat tied inside the cave.

Launching the boat was surprisingly easy. They pushed it into the shallow water and then flung themselves over the side. A pair of oars were lashed inside, and they each took one and rowed away from the beach. Within a few minutes a current caught them and the boat sliced effortlessly through the growing swells.

There was no wind, and although the moon silvered the cliff behind them, outlining the grim shape of Tregarth Hall, the horizon was lost in what appeared to be a low bank of cloud. Wisps of grey mist drifted over the surface of the sea.

"We must pull for the opposite shore now," Darcy said, but Gwyneth could not see the movement of her lips. Shipping her oar, Darcy shook Gwyneth's arm and pointed to the far side of the bay. In a moment, they would round the headland, and the cove that sheltered the Inn of the Blue Lantern would be visible.

Suddenly, a vivid column of fire shot up against the dark shore. They stared in surprise. Was the inn afire? Darcy wondered. She clutched Gwyneth's arm and pointed in the opposite direction, indicating that they had better avoid what could be a beacon fire lighting their way to capture.

They both pulled hard, but somehow the boat was no longer easy to propel. Instead of moving shoreward, they were now being pulled inexorably out to sea. After half an hour of struggling against the current, they could barely see the fire, and wisps of mist hanging over the water were becoming ominously thicker.

Soon everything was obscured by a blanket of fog. With no sense of direction, they stopped rowing and stared in dismay into the smothering grey curtain. The swells increased, and one rolling mountain of a wave drenched them with water, washing the oars overboard. They bailed water frantically while the boat was tossed about helplessly.

A cold dawn lightened the fog but did not penetrate deeply enough to show them the shore. They had shipped an alarming amount of water. Sliding down the fronts of swells, the unpredictable channel churned whitecaps and flung them in contemptuous circles. They were soaking wet and chilled to the marrow.

Then the fog lifted, driven shoreward by increasing winds. A huge swell formed, towering over the boat, sucking it broadside to the pinnacle. The next moment they capsized in a flurry of stinging spray and blown spume.

Darcy felt the shock of the icy water pulling her beneath its gunmetal surface. For a moment, she spun in a blurred world of swirling shadows, her lungs bursting; then her head popped out of the sea only feet away from the upturned boat.

She could feel her skirts dragging her down as she lunged toward the boat, kicking with all her might. Clinging to the sodden wood, she looked around wildly for Gwyneth, screaming her name as though she could hear. A moment later she saw her, struggling in the water a few yards away, obviously unable to swim.

Darcy fumbled with her skirts, ripping the material in her haste to be free. Her slippers were kicked off and floated away. Pushing off from the side of the boat, she swam to Gwyneth.

For a moment, she was afraid the girl's terrified flailing would drown them both. She managed to hook her arm under Gwyneth's chin and backstroke toward the boat.

A few minutes later, they clung to the overturned boat, searching the empty sea but unable to see either land or a rescuing vessel.

The cold brought an icy burning of limbs, teeth chattering, lips blue, wet hair plastered to dripping faces. How long did they hold on to the boat? Time was meaningless in the misery of cramped bodies and, strangely, insatiable thirst.

Gwyneth mouthed the words, "Tide will turn. Fishing boats come." But Darcy knew the boats would not be likely to put to sea in swells such as these.

How long could they survive before they succumbed to exposure? Darcy wondered. No, better not to think of that. But Gwyneth was right about one thing—they were now being pulled again by an unseen current. The movement of the boat was swift enough to be noticeable even from their waterlogged view.

They bobbed up over the top of a long swell, and land came into sight. Darcy wanted to shout with joy. She pointed, and Gwyneth looked over her shoulder and saw the long, dark line of shore. They both paddled with one hand while holding on to the boat with the other but soon realized it was better to let the current take them.

When they were within shouting distance of the shore, the pull of the current let them go and they floundered helplessly, washing back and forth but too far out for Darcy to swim with Gwyneth in tow.

Darcy wanted to scream. To be so close and yet unable to propel themselves to safety. A peculiar lethargy was replacing the former cramped coldness of her limbs, and she attempted to kick her feet to keep the circulation going, motioning for Gwyneth to do the same.

Then she looked up and saw the most beautiful sight in the world. A fishing trawler was headed directly for them.

Chapter Eleven

SIR LAURENCE HAD stirred on the chilled stone floor, groaning as the demon who pounded his skull continued to beat on his senses. Pushing himself up to his knees, he felt about him in the total darkness.

His hand closed over something cold and hard nearby. One of the iron masks. There was something else, something smaller. He picked it up and felt the torn fragment of cloth attached to it. An ornament of some kind from Darcy's dress, he decided, slipping it into his pocket.

A throbbing pain at the base of his skull and a feeling of disorientation seemed to be his only ailments. He swore loudly as he stood up, unsure of direction in the darkness. Why hadn't the stupid servants come to his aid? But of course, he had ordered them all back to bed.

Feeling his way carefully, he came to the rusted metal and ancient wood of the rack, then felt his way along the wall to the foot of the steps.

The servant girl, of course, he thought angrily as he started up the stairs. Gwyneth had come to her mistress's aid. He would take pleasure in whipping the girl personally before he had her flung into prison. Attempted murder would guarantee that the little wretch would, at the very least, be sent to a penal colony for life. She could hang for the act if it were proved to be premeditated.

And Darcy . . . he'd make her pay dearly for this humiliation. They would have taken the boat since they would have been stopped if they had attempted to cross the bridge to the mainland.

He smiled grimly at that folly. They would exhaust themselves fighting the current, which would simply pull them out to sea and then, when the tide turned, bring them back. He was near the top of the stairs now and impatient to see what had happened to the two women.

A rat darted across his foot. He felt the loathsome creature's body brush against his ankle. He kicked blindly and missed the rat but connected with the top of the next step, causing him to stumble. For a second, he clutched at the air; then he felt his foot slip over the edge and he was falling. A moment later everything rushed away in a great explosion of pain.

Cullen awakened from a drunken sleep and went looking for his father after the servants had reported that Sir Laurence had not appeared for breakfast and no, they had not seen Miss Darcy either. The mute, Gwyneth, was nowhere to be found.

When he had searched everywhere else, Cullen went reluctantly down to the cellar. Surely his father had not stayed down in the dungeon all night? Cullen had drunk himself to sleep to shut out the picture of Darcy's face as she was being taken to the dungeon, telling himself that the little fool deserved to be punished.

Cullen's head ached, and his stomach churned from the night's drinking. He walked unsteadily to the top of the flight of stairs, holding a lantern aloft and stamping his feet to warn off any lurking rats.

He stood looking down for several seconds before his eyes found the body of his father at the foot of the stone stairs.

There was no doubt from the angle of the neck and the wide staring eyes that Sir Laurence Tregarth was dead.

The fishing trawler that plucked Darcy and Gwyneth from the sea put in to the nearest cove to put them ashore. Their ordeal ended in front of a blazing fire at the Inn of the Blue Lantern.

Wrapped in blankets and sipping hot cocoa, they soon gathered from the conversation of the innkeeper and his daughter that someone had set several fishing boats afire the previous night, no doubt to warn off Captain Stede Winslow, who was known to be bringing a cargo of wine to the inn.

"You two wouldn't have had something to do with those fires, would you now?" Albert asked them suspiciously.

"Now, Albert," one of the rescuing fishermen protested, "How could they have started the fires when they were clinging to a boat out in the bay? You heard what they said; they were running away from Tregarth Hall. And I for one don't blame them. Strange ones, those Tregarths. Father and son, both of them. Should have stayed in those heathen islands, Sir Laurence should."

A young man with delicately handsome features, light blue eyes, and a shy smile, limped toward them, relying heavily on a cane to assist him. He dragged a lifeless foot, Darcy noted, but somehow managed a sweeping bow when he reached them. He was looking at Darcy as though he recognized her and at the same time found it hard to resist staring at Gwyneth.

"Forgive me, mam'selle," he said in flawless but accented English. "Allow me to present myself. I am Philippe Givet. Did we meet in France mam'selle?" he asked Darcy.

"Why—no. I've never been there. I am Darcy Sinclair and this is—" she paused, deciding that Gwyneth was hardly a servant any longer. "My friend, Gwyneth." Darcy had never known Gwyneth's last name so added, "Jones. Miss Jones is mute, but she will understand the movement of your lips if you speak slowly and make sure she can see your face."

"*Enchanté*, mam'selle." Philippe bent to kiss Darcy's hand, then took Gwyneth's tiny hand in his and seemed most reluctant to relinquish it.

"Ah, now I remember," Philippe said. "Your portrait. I

have seen your portrait. It is hanging—'' he stopped, glancing about the inn as he realized others were listening. "I'm sorry. I was mistaken,'' he added hastily.

"I could not help but overhear of your plight,'' Philippe went on. "And came to offer my room. You could rest there, dry your clothing, and perhaps decide what to do next.''

Darcy had been wondering how she would pay Albert for the hot cocoa and how long she and Gwyneth could linger in the public saloon before someone sent word to Tregarth Hall. The young Frenchman was obviously a gentleman of high birth, and there was something about his sad eyes that said he had known great suffering himself. She decided to take a chance. "We would be most grateful,'' she said.

When Philippe opened the door to his room, Darcy almost cried out in surprise as she recognized the bookshelves beside the fireplace. It was the same room she had been in that first night at the inn. She drew back momentarily, half expecting Stede Winslow to come through the revolving panel.

"Something is wrong?'' Philippe asked. "Please, have no fear. I shall withdraw at once and leave you alone. But first, I wanted to tell you, privately, that I am aware that Captain Winslow has a portrait of you aboard his ship. Since you are obviously close to him, I must tell you that I owe him my life and would gladly die for him or for his lady.''

Darcy's mouth opened in surprise. "I believe we had better tell each other more about Captain Winslow,'' she said.

Philippe persuaded Violet to part with one of her skirts to replace the one Darcy had lost at sea and ordered a hearty meal to be sent up to them. Gwyneth dried the rest of their clothes in front of the fire. When Philippe returned they were fed and dressed. Two hours later, they had exchanged stories of their acquaintance with Stede.

"The Excise officers have just returned,'' he said. "They believe Stede slipped ashore last night in a small boat although his ship did not come in.'' Philippe was careful to turn his face toward Gwyneth as he spoke. Gwyneth watched him with a shy smile and heightened color in her cheeks.

Gwyneth's eyes suddenly widened, and she clutched Darcy in fright. Following her gaze, they saw the bookshelves revolve. Stede stepped through the apperture. "I'm indebted to you for the beacon fire, Philippe," he said, bowing to Darcy. "Had I known you had such charming company, I would have been here sooner." To Darcy he said, "I trust your presence here means you have left Tregarth?"

"Most dramatically," Philippe said. "They have just been plucked from the sea."

Darcy related what had happened, adding, "If we're caught, I'm afraid there will be assault charges brought against us."

Stede said, "Then you must allow me to place my ship at your disposal. She is sailing along the coast until I signal her."

"Captain Winslow, you presume too much—" Darcy protested.

Ignoring the presence of the others, Stede spoke rapidly and urgently to Darcy alone. "Come to America with me. I've fulfilled my promise to my uncle—all of the family are now safe in England. Darcy, follow that impetuous streak in your nature that shines from your eyes. Come to a young, new country and be whatever you will.

"Indebted to Stede Winslow, for one thing," Darcy retorted.

"You'll never be indebted to anyone again. I've brought you a legacy from France—it's aboard my ship. I regret that I also bring you the news that your grandmother is dead."

"I never knew her . . . but I'm so sorry."

"There's nothing to keep you here. If you aren't afraid for yourself then think of Gwyneth," Stede urged.

"I would be happy to offer my protection to Mam'selle Gwyneth," Philippe offered, trying valiantly to bring his heels together as he gave a stiff bow.

Darcy looked from one to the other. She wanted to follow her heart and tell Stede Winslow she would happily accompany him to the far side of the earth, but an inner voice urged caution. "Would my grandmother's bequest be enough to pay passage for myself and Gwyneth to America?"

Stede laughed. "It's almost enough to *buy* America," he began but was interrupted by a commotion in the courtyard below. They heard the clatter of horses' hooves and a shout for Albert to show himself. Stede raised the window slightly and looked out, gesturing for the others to keep out of sight.

Cullen Tregarth and three of his men pranced about the courtyard impatiently as Albert and several Excise officers came through the door. Cullen raised his hand and threw something to the ground at the feet of the nearest officer.

"Look at it, man. It is the family crest of the Winslows. He has been here—slipped right through your net, you fools. I found that buckle near the murdered body of my father."

Darcy gasped, her hand going to her waist where she had fastened Stede's buckle. She thought she had lost it at sea. "Murdered. . . ." she whispered. "But we thought he was only unconscious."

Cullen was shouting. "What are you waiting for? Search every inch of ground. Every cottage and cave. Don't forget the church. I want this inn taken apart, stone by stone. Find him. A hundred sovereigns for the man who brings me Stede Winslow."

Stede closed the window silently. "Philippe, take the ladies to safety down the passage I showed you. After dark, signal my ship. Three long flashes of light, two short."

Philippe looked from Stede to Gwyneth and Darcy, torn between the desire to stay with Stede and the urgent need to take the women away. It was hard to believe that the diminutive Gwyneth had clubbed her employer to death.

"But what of you, Stede, what will you do?"

"I'll lead Tregarth on a merry chase. Go now—quickly." He pushed the panel behind the bookshelves, and they stepped into a room used for the storage of linens, chamber pots, and lanterns.

Philippe opened a trapdoor in the floor as Stede disappeared from view. Gwyneth was half way down a ladder, and Darcy had begun to descend when Philippe heard pounding on the doors along the landing. A voice yelled, "There he is! After him!"

"I must go back," Philippe said to Darcy. "Perhaps I can create a diversion—help Stede escape. You go on—wait for us on the beach." Without waiting for a reply, he dropped the trapdoor over their heads.

But Stede had not shown Philippe how to activate the revolving wall, and he wasted precious minutes before realizing he could simply walk out of the door leading to the landing. By the time he had dragged his withered foot down the stairs to the courtyard, the Excise men were dragging Stede away, his hands tied behind his back. At almost the same instant, Darcy and Gwyneth were stumbling from the fish cellar into the waiting arms of another group of officers.

Chapter Twelve

CULLEN TREGARTH STOOD with his back to the roaring fire, a footman nearby, ready to leap to do his bidding should he need his brandy glass refilled, another log thrown on the fire, his snuff box held. Cullen was well satisfied with most of the day's events.

Winslow was chained in the dungeon. None of the villagers had dared challenge Cullen's decision to keep the prisoner in his own home. The man had slipped through the fingers of the Customs and Excise officers too many times.

Cullen thought with some pleasure that it might take days, even weeks, for the magistrate to arrive. Winslow would have plenty of time to regret falling into Tregarth hands. There were many old scores to settle, and a hangman's noose would be too quick and merciful.

When Cullen's anger over his father's death had subsided, he realized that what he felt was not grief. He had always been secretly afraid of his father. Nor was there any reason to deny to himself that he was enjoying his new position in the world as master of Tregarth Hall, its tenant farms and acres of land . . . dependent though they were on the rather immediate arrival of Evadne's dowry and the D'Arcy jewels. His father had borrowed heavily, using the hall as collateral, and the prospect of soon to be acquired wealthy brides.

The butler entered the room, coughed discreetly, and said, "Forgive the intrusion, sir, but the Lady Evadne has arrived."

He had barely uttered the words than Evadne fluttered into the room like a tiny white moth in her white satin gown trimmed with swansdown.

"Cullen . . . I just heard," she cried brokenly. "Where is he?"

"My father's body is—" Cullen began.

"No, no! I can't bear to hear of him," Evadne said. "Tell me, where is the smuggler who murdered him? Where is Winslow? I shall have him whipped before the law takes him. They said you brought him here." Her eyes were wild with grief, her tiny fists clenched over her bosom.

Cullen looked into her eyes, eyes that were glittering like a cat's. "Why my dear Evadne, such vengeance. One would almost imagine that it had been I . . . your intended husband . . . who had been murdered."

"Oh, you milksop," Evadne stormed. "If you were half the man your father was. . . ." She raised her fist as though to strike him, and Cullen caught her wrist.

"So it was true. You shared my father's bed. Tell me, why did he not marry you himself and allow me to marry Darcy? What a great deal of trouble we should all have been spared."

She glared up at him, all pretense of helpless femininity erased. Her hand jerked loose, and she raked her fingernails down his face. Cullen fingered the red marks on his cheek.

"Damn you," Evadne screamed. "Why couldn't it have been you the smuggler killed. Do you think I'll marry you now? I'd rather be dead. The only reason I consented in the first place was because my father was so opposed to Laurence. The only reason I would allow a fumbling boy like you to touch me was so that I could be near a real man. . . . Yes, I loved your father. You . . . you can go to hell." She turned and ran from the room.

Cullen watched her go, making no attempt to follow. He motioned for the impassive footman to fill his glass, then sprawled in the leather armchair beside the fire and sipped his brandy thoughtfully.

The Tregarth debts were monumental. He and his father had both always been fonder of the gaming tables than was good for family finances. His father had spent a great deal putting the ancestral home in a livable condition. Without Evadne's dowry, he could lose everything. Unless Darcy could be persuaded that he had jilted Evadne because he loved Darcy. He had kept her locked in her room because of the ridiculous story she told, explaining to everyone that she was overwrought. He would talk to her, concoct a story to convince her that he loved her. Then they would bring her grandmother—and her wealth—from France.

Dressed in a black gown with a black lace cap on her head, Darcy sat stiffly in the drawing room, part of a somber circle of mourners who had just returned from the funeral service. Sipping sherry, Darcy shook her head as a footman approached with a tray of seedcake. Evadne was weeping quietly in a corner while Cullen accepted condolences from a long line of visitors.

Darcy was bewildered by Cullen's abrupt change of attitude. He refused to believe that she had hit his father with an iron mask. Darcy had made no mention of Gwyneth's part in their escape. Cullen had stared at her, giving a derisive laugh. "You? Overpowered my father? Come on, Darcy, do you take me for a fool?" His dark eyes narrowed, lids descending in a way frighteningly reminiscent of his father's hooded gaze. "You're protecting that swine Winslow. Why?"

He caught her wrist, dragging her closer to him. "If you repeat that ridiculous story to anyone, I shall have you and that useless mute you're so fond of put away. You'll do as you're told, Darcy, or unpleasant things will happen, I promise you. My father gave you too much rein. You're too spirited and imaginative for your own good. And damned opinionated for a woman." His eyes had gleamed like evil mirrors.

There had been no reasoning with him. After making these threats, he had suddenly professed his love for her, even going down on one knee to ask her to marry him.

"What about Evadne?" she asked.

"Surely you didn't imagine I would marry her now? It was father's wish, never mine. You are my only true love. You can't have forgotten all we shared? The times I visited you at school? Do you remember the time I took you to the zoo? And the little tea shop where the absent-minded proprietor kept bringing more and more eclairs?"

"But you agreed to marry Evadne," Darcy protested.

"Sacrificing myself in order to save you from father's wrath. Darling, I never dared tell you, but he treated your mother abominably. He tricked her into going to the Indies. She thought they were merely going for a short honeymoon cruise, but the ship was bound for Jamaica. Your mother did not want to leave you behind in England. Besides, she had made that terrible journey before when she ran away with Geoffrey Winslow and ended up marrying the ship's captain Sinclair. She knew how unhealthy the climate was—she knew of the constant epidemics of yellow fever."

"Yes," Darcy said grimly. "I have read a great deal on the subject of yellow fever since my mother died of it."

"My father had a strange twisted compulsion to make her go back there because she had spurned him for Winslow. He never forgave her for that."

"But—why did she marry him?" Darcy asked. "Cullen, I was so young when she went away; there is so much I don't know."

"She was in desperate financial straits, a widow trying to support a young daughter, when my father found her again. You knew he had been one of her suitors when she was a girl, but she refused him? He promised that if she married him he would pay for your education and arrange a reconciliation with her mother, who was by this time also a widow and, as it turned out, a recluse."

Darcy understood her mother's desperation. There were so few ways open to a woman to support herself and a child. Eventually, Darcy had agreed to remain silent about her part in Sir

Laurence's death in exchange for being allowed the freedom of Tregarth Hall.

As Darcy watched the funeral guests conversing in small groups, she was waiting for an opportunity to slip down to the dungeons.

Evadne was still weeping uncontrollably. At last, one of the other women led her away to a private room. Evadne's father, his face grim, promptly approached Cullen, and the two of them disappeared into the study.

Darcy stood up, glancing about to see if anyone was watching her. Quietly, she slipped out into the hall, and after a brief stop in the kitchen to pick up a pitcher of water, made her way down to the dungeons.

One of the burlier grooms was guarding the stone steps, sitting with his back to the wall, a pistol on his lap. He scrambled to his feet when Darcy approached.

"Stand aside," Darcy ordered.

He touched his forelock. "Begging your pardon, Mistress, but I was ordered by the Master not to let anyone pass."

"Has the prisoner been given water today?" Darcy inquired icily, staring the man down.

"No—but—"

"Stand aside then. You can see I have only a pitcher of water. Tell me, how would you like to be down there for a day and a night without water? It is inhuman."

The man hesitated, unnerved by the resolve in the young woman's gaze. Her eyes seemed to flash a golden fire in their spice-brown depths, like a lioness about to spring. He stood aside.

Darcy went as quickly down the stone steps as the uncertain surface would allow. Stede was manacled to the wall. Surely, she thought as she hurried to Stede's side, such medieval barbarism must be against the law. But in this remote spot she supposed the Tregarths were a law unto themselves.

Stede's black hair hung over his face, his head was slumped forward on his chest and, when she drew near, she saw to her horror that his shirt had been ripped from his back and a criss-cross pattern of welts oozed blood. Hearing her footsteps, he raised his head. The pain in his eyes made her throat constrict, but he gave her a hint of a grin.

"Mistress Darcy Sinclair," he murmured through cracked lips. "So they caught you too. . . . "

Darcy pressed the pitcher to his lips, not trusting herself to speak for fear she would dissolve into tears of both compassion and anger. How could one human being do this to another? How could Cullen do it? What had become of the handsome, teasing young man who had set schoolgirls' hearts fluttering? No, it was impossible, Cullen must not be aware of this. She shivered, glancing over her shoulder, half expecting the ghost of Sir Laurence to materialize. This brutality was more his style.

When Stede had finished drinking, Darcy placed the pitcher on the floor and tore a strip from her petticoat. Dampening it with the remainder of the water, she gently cleaned the blood from Stede's back. He did not wince.

"I tried to tell him you didn't kill his father," she whispered.

"Don't implicate yourself. You must leave here. Cullen Tregarth is like his father. If he's thwarted in any way it brings out a streak of madness. He's already boasted that he will marry you, Darcy."

"I can't leave while you are here—"

"You must. It's urgent that you take a message to Philippe. Knowing my gallant young friend, he will be planning some impossible escape for me single-handedly. Tell him to signal my ship and bring her in so that my crew can help."

The guard appeared at the top of the steps and called, "You be all right down there milady?"

"I must go—I will take the message to Philippe," Darcy said.

"Wait a moment," Stede said. "There may not be another chance for a while for me to tell you of my feelings for you. Tell me you feel an answering spark—that you've thought of me, not as much as I've thought of you perhaps—but a little? Darcy, perhaps we're destined to fulfill the lost promises of my father and your mother." The effort to speak brought perspiration to his brow, and his flesh burned with fever under her ministering hands.

"This is neither the time nor the place to discuss such things," Darcy said, but a little flutter of happiness went through her. She bent to pick up the pitcher.

"At least promise to come to America. I've acquired a substantial fortune of my own. I tell you this in case you suspect my motives."

"You're quite mad," Darcy said, "but I will go with you to America." Out of the corner of her eye she could see the guard hovering nervously. Stede gave her one last grateful glance as she went quickly back up to the funeral guests.

In the study, Lord Dunforth faced a tight-lipped Cullen. "I don't believe it," Cullen said. "The girl Gwyneth is mute. How could she communicate with anyone?"

"She reads and writes; someone taught her," Lord Dunforth said. "She took her story to the physician who examined your father's body."

"And where is the mute now?"

"We don't know. She disappeared after leaving her written confession in the physician's hands."

"I don't believe a word of it. Winslow broke into the house once before. And I found his buckle beside my father's body. You don't understand. The Winslows and Tregarths—it goes back a long time. If I don't destroy Winslow now, he will surely destroy me."

"Cullen, for God's sake be reasonable. If Winslow goes on trial for murder of your father, all sorts of dirty linen will be aired. Not least of which is my daughter's association with your father. Evadne is so grief-stricken I fear she will make some sort of public declaration at the trial. Listen to me, Cullen, the physician is prepared to write 'accidental death' on the certificate. The magistrate has not yet been summoned. The whole thing can be hushed up.''

"And what about Winslow? What becomes of him?''

"He is still guilty of smuggling. Of course, there's no guarantee he'll hang for it.''

Cullen walked across the room, leaned on the mantelpiece, and stared into the flames of the fire. A triangular piece of blackened wood slipped to the red hot embers and was consumed in a spurt of flame. "Have you heard about the new means of dispatching criminals in France?'' he asked. "An ingenious invention they call the guillotine. While I was in Paris last April they executed the first robber. An almost silent death. There are only three sounds, and those are muffled. The sound of the plank—with the victim tied to it—being slid into place. Then the yoke holding the head is closed. Lastly, the swift descent of the knife.''

Lord Dunforth shuddered as Cullen turned slowly to face him, his eyes gleaming. Dunforth was glad that Evadne had announced she would not marry Cullen. Looking at Tregarth's son, Lord Dunforth saw now that he was merely a younger version of his father. Already, there were suggestions of sadism and instability.

Cullen said, "Did you know that Winslow's mother was a French noblewoman? His uncle was very close to the king until an affair of the heart sent him into self-imposed exile in America.''

"What exactly are you driving at?'' Lord Dunforth asked.

"You want my father's death quietly forgotten. I want Winslow to pay for it. There is a solution. If we can arrange for him to go to France, delivered into the hands of the Revolutionary Tribunal and with evidence that his family exploited the peasants and he himself is a counterrevolutionary, he will die.''

Lord Dunforth considered this silently, thinking of Evadne's hysterical grief and wild threats. His daughter was as convinced as Cullen that Winslow had killed her lover. "It would be relatively easy to place Winslow on a fishing boat that would take him to France," he said slowly. "You could say he escaped. That's what everyone expects him to do."

"Four men, at least," Cullen said. "And Winslow in chains all the way, to be sure. Tonight—he must be sent to France tonight."

Chapter Thirteen

DARCY SEARCHED EVERYWHERE for Gwyneth. No one had seen her. Nor could Darcy inquire of Cullen, for he had also disappeared shortly after dinner.

The funeral guests had departed, and an uneasy stillness had fallen upon the house. Servants crept about, lighting lanterns, fueling fires, warming beds, then vanishing back to their own quarters. Darcy was anxious to find her way to the Inn of the Blue Lantern, but she was loathe to leave until she knew what had happened to Gwyneth.

When the activities of the servants ceased, Darcy went to the kitchens. Two scullery maids were washing the last of the pots used for dinner. The cook, butler, and other servants were now enjoying their own evening meal in the servants' hall.

The two young girls looked at her with heavy eyes. Darcy said quietly, "Go about your business. I will see to my own needs." The maids were too exhausted from their day's labor to show more than a passing interest in the lady of the house and her enormous appetite; for, after having consumed a seven-course dinner, she was now collecting bread, cheese, and cold meat.

Darcy wrapped a linen serviette around the food and took it straight down to the dungeon. A lantern was burning at the top of the stone steps, but there was no sign of a guard. Puzzled, Darcy approached slowly, looking over her shoulder to see if the shadows concealed a lurking figure.

Stede was gone. The dungeons were empty.

Philippe, Darcy thought. I must go to Philippe at once. She ran back up to her chambers. Could Stede have escaped? Surely she would have heard the alarm. She was fumbling in her wardrobe for her warmest clothes when she found Gwyneth's note pinned to her cloak and out of sight of the prying eyes of any chambermaid who might enter the room.

"Must tell truth. Stede cannot hang," Gwyneth had written.

Darcy held the note, considering. It would take too long to reach the inn on foot; it was simply too far and too hilly. With Cullen gone and with her new status in the house, who would stop her from leaving? She changed quickly into her riding habit.

Like the house servants, the grooms and stable boys were all busy with their evening meal. No one saw her take her favorite mare, throw on a saddle, and lead her into the courtyard.

The moon had not yet risen, and the bridge leading to the mainland was dark. When she had led the mare half way across and no shout from the watchtower stayed her progress, Darcy climbed into the saddle and urged the mare into a canter, glad that since Sir Laurence's death security practices had been forgotten.

In the cobblestoned courtyard of the inn, as she was approaching the blue circle of light cast by the lantern, a cloaked figure on a black horse loomed out of the shadows, seizing her reins. Her mare, pressed to the flanks of the second horse, whinnied and began to rear in fright. Darcy raised her riding crop to ward off her attacker. In the last second before she struck his face, she recognized Philippe.

"Oh, Philippe, you frightened me—"

"Quickly, come this way," Philippe said, guiding her horse with his own.

They rode along the narrow lane, climbed the hill, and stopped on the rocky bluff overlooking a tiny inlet in the jagged coastline.

"We thought you would come after Tregarth and his men

appeared at the inn and commissioned one of Albert's fishing boats. What is happening at Tregarth Hall, and what news of Stede?''

Darcy told him breathlessly that both Stede and Gwyneth had disappeared.

''Gwyneth is safe. She is waiting in a secret room at the inn. I thought it better not to let you enter the inn because two of Tregarth's men are still in the saloon. I have been waiting in the courtyard since Tregarth left. *Dieu* . . . I see now what he is about, and I allowed it to happen.''

Philippe's horse pranced restlessly in the shadows, and Darcy was struck by the fact that Philippe seemed almost a part of his mount. He was transformed from a frail young man with a withered foot to a splendidly competent horseman, his limp and his cane forgotten.

''I don't understand,'' Darcy said. ''Allowed what to happen?''

''Gwyneth has confessed that it was she who struck the blow that killed Tregarth. She came to me at the inn after giving a written confession to the physician. I intended to slip her aboard Stede's ship tonight.

''Don't you see, Darcy? Because of the confession, Stede could not be convicted of Sir Laurence's murder, and Cullen would be deprived of the sort of bloody revenge that would satisfy him. In my poor tormented country, it is easy to falsely accuse a man, bring him swiftly to trial—the outcome assured —and place him in a tumbril for that last journey to Madame Guillotine. In Stede's case, he could be convicted of smuggling *aristos* out of the country—myself included. To say nothing of his own royal blood line.''

''You believe Cullen has transported him to France? Oh, Philippe, what can we do now?''

''In a little while we shall light a lantern and signal Stede's ship. I shall then sail for France to see what I can do.''

''Take me with you,'' Darcy said at once. ''And Gwyneth

too. We can't stay here now, or Gwyneth will surely be caught.''

"Then we shall board Stede's ship," Philippe agreed. "And now we must send the signal.''

They waited at the edge of the sea, hidden by the rocks, and watched the silent silhouette of the *Tawny Rose* glide into the cove. A moment later, there was a faint splash as a small boat hit the water.

Philippe held Gwyneth's hand tightly as she stepped into the shallow water to climb into the boat. When she was safely aboard, he turned to help Darcy. A few minutes later, Chalmers helped the two women climb up the rope ladder over the side of the ship.

The *Tawny Rose* was slicing through the dark swells of the Channel before Philippe had finished explaining to the first officer what had happened to Stede.

Chalmers looked at the two women standing on deck. "Ship's fast becoming a ladies' hostel," he growled. "Countrywoman of yours still aboard. These two will have to share her cabin.''

"My countrywoman?" Philippe repeated, puzzled.

"Come," Chalmers said. "She wouldn't budge. Waiting for the captain.''

Darcy followed the others to the captain's cabin with a sense of foreboding. Her fears were fully realized when the gruff first officer pushed open the cabin door. An exotically lovely young woman lay on the captain's bunk, a handkerchief pressed to her lips. Despite her obvious distress at the rolling of the ship, she was flamboyantly pretty, with flaring nostrils and expressive dark eyes matched by a cloud of wavy hair.

"Miss Corinne Dubois," Chalmers said, and promptly departed.

Corinne glared at her unexpected visitors. "What are you doing aboard the *Tawny Rose?*" she demanded, hands clutching at her stomach as the ship rolled again.

"The *Tawny Rose*...." Darcy repeated. "That is the name of Stede's ship?"

Peering at Darcy, Corinne struggled to sit up. "Turn up the lantern," she said. "I cannot see you."

Philippe turned up the wick of the lantern hanging from the bulkhead. Corinne gave an audible gasp. "You ... you are the tawny rose." Her voice was shrill, and she attempted to get out of the bunk, but the vessel lurched and she sank back.

"Who are you?" Darcy asked. "And what do you know of the tawny rose?"

"I am Captain Stede Winslow's woman," Corinne said. "And when I recover from the *mal de mer*, I will probably scratch your eyes out. Then I will kill you."

Mercifully, first officer Chalmers was prevailed upon to relinquish his cabin to Darcy and Gwyneth for the rest of the night. Darcy stood in his cabin, which was even smaller than the captain's, and gazed at the portrait of her mother, so often talked about but never seen.

It was like looking into a ghostly mirror. Darcy's misty memory of her mother had been of a beautiful woman with a coquettish allure who loved to dress up and dance and laugh. Playful and charming and not very practical. Darcy had always felt that she was probably more like her father, John Sinclair, than her mother.

But now she was sure that her physical resemblance to her mother had grown uncanny since she had reached womanhood. It was little wonder that Stede had been so taken aback upon seeing her for the first time at the inn.

Gwyneth kept looking from Darcy to the portrait, shaking her head in bewilderment. In the background of the picture was an imposing French chateau, and the hairstyle and clothes were at least twenty years out of date, but to Gwyneth's eyes the subject appeared to be Darcy.

The portrait showed such a young and vulnerable Regine. Her eyes seemed to shine in the dim light of the cabin as though bright with tears. She appeared to be beseeching someone who stood behind the artist who painted her . . . could it have been Geoffrey Winslow . . . about to marry another woman?

Darcy felt her own eyes misting as she contemplated the tragic destinies of her mother and Geoffrey Winslow. It was some time before she remembered that Stede had installed Corinne Dubois in his own cabin and that Corinne was a flesh and blood woman who had made her relationship to Stede very clear.

When the *Tawny Rose* arrived at a small fishing village in Normandy, the three women were left aboard with the crew while Philippe rode into Paris to learn what had become of Stede. After the first day of bobbing about at anchor, Corinne went ashore and did not return. Darcy and Gwyneth remained below decks and waited.

Three days later, Philippe returned, looking haggard and disheveled. "He is not in the Temple," he said. "He was transferred to the *Conciergerie*."

"You know the place?" Darcy asked.

"A gloomy building that was formerly a royal dining hall and storehouse—on the Ile St. Louis on the Seine. It is being used as a prison because it is next door to the Palais de Justice. Stede is in a cell with fifty others . . . with only straw to sleep on, fighting for a mouthful of slops a dog would not eat."

"You sound as though you know what it is like in that awful place," Darcy put in.

Philippe gave her a sad little half smile. "I did not see him but was told he has been ill with fever. The whiplashes on his back festered. One of the other prisoners treated him, and it is hoped he will soon be well enough to go to the guillotine."

Darcy covered her face with her hands. Philippe said quickly, "Don't despair. We stand a better chance of getting him out of the *Conciergerie* than if he were in the Temple, from which there is no escape. The Temple is a prison of unscalable towers with narrow slits for windows and is surrounded by a deep ditch. The *Conciergerie*, on the other hand, constantly has a crowd of people milling about on the stairs waiting for victims to be taken down to the tumbrils."

Chalmers had listened silently. Now he said, "We are too few to break into a prison in the middle of Paris."

Philippe limped to the cabin table and sat down. "Perhaps it won't be necessary. Bring me food, please, and wine. I have documents to prepare, letters to write." He looked up at them with an almost roguish smile. "Most of which will be forgeries to ensure our safe passage about the city. But first, I must write to my former employer . . . Francois–Maximilien–Joseph Isidore Robespierre."

"Robespierre!" Darcy and Chalmers said in unison.

"Philippe—surely you did not work for that monster?" Darcy cried.

"He was not always as bloodthirsty as he is now," Philippe said. "And even now, one can't argue with his ideals. But I must confess that I never anticipated this bloodbath. I was a student when he was still a lawyer. I helped when he was elected to the National Assembly as a deputy of the Third Estate for Artois. I wrote pamphlets for him. I admired Robespierre because he was dedicated to the teachings of Rousseau just as I was. He knew my father was a marquis. I was stupid, I suppose, to believe that my lineage did not matter to Robespierre. I must surely have represented all that he despised. The first hint of betrayal among his followers and it was I who was accused. I was innocent . . . and despite my imprisonment and torture, I have not changed my views. The revolution was necessary. The day we stormed the Bastille will live as the greatest day in our history."

Philippe was writing as he spoke. Gwyneth crouched on the other side of the table, watching his lips and occasionally allowing her glance to wander over his face and caress his delicate long fingers as they wielded the quill with sure strokes.

"What do you intend to do?" Darcy asked.

"I shared a cell with Stede's cousin. Stede came at night, overpowered one of the guards and donned his clothing. But we two were in a private cell thanks to the bribes of our families. Stede is in a communal cell with many guards, so we cannot get him out by force."

"Then what . . . " Darcy began.

"I am writing to Robespierre to offer myself for Stede. I know he would rather feed me to the guillotine than a foreigner whose only crime is that he smuggled a few *aristos* out of the country. I, after all, am a traitor—or at least Robespierre believes that I am."

Gwyneth leaped to her feet, her face stricken. She clutched at Philippe's arm to stop him from writing.

Darcy said, "I'm sure Stede would never agree to such a plan. Besides, you have no guarantee Robespierre would honor such an exchange. You might both find yourselves riding the tumbrils."

Philippe slowly crumpled the letter between his fingers. "Then we shall visit the *Conciergerie*. I will wear my cape over torn and dirty clothing. Amid fifty prisoners it should be easy enough to give the cloak to Stede and take his place. If two of us were to enter and two leave, the guards might not notice. Especially if Stede took my cane and affected a limp. It is, alas, my most distinguishing feature."

"Enough," Chalmers said irritably. "Cap'n never let another man die for him. Been thinking—cap'n good at tricky climbs. Seen him go up rigging when it were torn apart in a storm and no other man dared climb."

"I take it you have a plan, m'sieur?"

"Reckless enough to appeal to my cap'n," Chalmers confirmed. "With some chance for success."

Chapter Fourteen

STEDE LAY IN the filthy straw of the communal cell in the *Conciergerie*.

His trial had been swiftly concluded and sentence passed. As a counterrevolutionary and a foreign agitator linked by blood to the French aristocracy, he would go to the guillotine.

All morning they had listened to the dread sound of tumbrils rattling through the streets to the jeers of the watching crowd.

Stede had been told by fellow prisoners that sometimes, in the case of a particularly interesting candidate for the steel caress of Madame Guillotine, the tumbril would be paraded up and down several streets before going back to the *Place de la Revolution*. This gave the watchers time to scream their assessment of the condemned, denouncing them as assassins, brigands, agents of tyranny, or throat cutters.

Some went to the guillotine indifferently, scornfully ignoring the mob; others sobbed for mercy while more than a few reacted with crowd-pleasing bravado, joking with the guards and the people lining the streets.

Female victims often worried more about their appearance than their imminent execution, asking for rouge for pale cheeks, a cap to cover their shaved hair.

These preliminary rides in the tumbrils were necessary, Stede learned, because of the blood lust of the crowds. The guillotine itself was so quick that it afforded little satisfaction to the watchers.

The prisoner who had helped Stede recover from a fever and

who had treated the torn flesh of his back was an elderly doctor whose hands retained their skill while his mind began to wander. He had laughed with glee as he told Stede, "The joke, m'sieur, is on the Revolutionary Tribunal. You see, I am already dead. Well, dying—I have only a few weeks left, perhaps only days."

He was doubled up with internal misery, and the rag he pressed to his lips was stained with blood. After a long paroxysm of coughing, he went on. "Now that we are sentenced, it will be purely a matter of chance. The jailors are drunk much of the time and often take the wrong prisoners. They call the names of those who are to die each day, and if there are two of the same name, they simply take both. Tell me your name, my young friend, so that if it is called first I may take your place. You have been kind, listening to an old man's ramblings. That would be a good joke to play. . . . "

Stede said gently, "I can't let you do that, sir. There is always a chance of reprieve."

"Reprieve! Never! I won't stand for it," the doctor gasped, coughing again. "I welcome an end to this misery. Do you know . . . I had dealings with Sanson, the executioner. Why, only days ago he complained to me that the two carts of his own were no longer enough to transport the condemned. He has had to hire others. His expenses, he says, are heavy. Ropes to bind the prisoners, wood and nails for scaffolding, wicker baskets to catch the heads. Do you know, he complained because he is not allowed to keep the clothes of his victims."

"Doctor—of what are you accused?" Stede asked to cut short this grisly recital.

The elderly man looked bewildered, scratched his thinning hair and then shrugged. "I have forgotten. I believe I may have treated a patient who was a counterrevolutionary."

As the day dragged on, the old doctor's ramblings grew less and less coherent. That night, to Stede's intense relief, the old man died quietly in his sleep.

The following morning, the guards burst into the cell to read the names of the day's victims. Prisoners stirred, muttering, those in chains rattling them. Near the end of the list, the guard stumbled over the unfamiliar English name.

"Win . . . Win—Winslow."

Stede's hair was shaved from the back of his head. His hands were tied behind him with rope. Then he was taken down the stairs, past crowds of men and women who craned their necks for a glimpse of those about to die.

The people on the streets waiting for the tumbrils to pass their way on route to the *Place de la Revolution* were startled by the appearance of a young man on horseback who rode erratically into the middle of the square shouting slogans.

He wore a flowing cape and looked suspiciously aristocratic, with pale finely chiseled features and long expressive fingers that he waved as he spoke. "Citizens . . . listen to me. For the bourgeoisie, the revolution is a matter of politics," he cried, his horse prancing as though leading a parade. "But for the people, it is a matter of economics."

"Is he drunk?" someone shouted. "What is he talking about?" Among the women watching there was a ripple of fear for the handsome young man who was surely inviting disaster. The tumbrils would pass this way at any moment.

"He is so pale—he must be ill," one matron declared.

Philippe shouted, "Is not famine still rampant? Can you eat the severed heads? You—and you—do you not go to your beds early because there are no candles to light your homes?

The crowd's attention was riveted on Philippe as he exhorted them to demand an end to the butchery, to demand a concentration on the needs of the citizens. He paraded his horse about the square, then cantered down the narrow street leading to the guillotine, followed by a curious group of hecklers.

Few of them noticed that a rope had been stretched between the upper story windows over their heads. One of the women saw the rope but surmised that the shopkeepers below had put it there, perhaps to hang rugs or laundry from, she thought, turning her attention back to the mad agitator on horseback. One of the men saw the rope too, and he remembered that the printer who owned the shop below was an odd fellow who in the early days of the revolution had hung political posters across the street.

A shout went up announcing that the first of the tumbrils was approaching. The crowd moved to the sidewalks, clearing the way. They could hear the wheels of the tumbril grinding a dirge on the pavements, and an expectant hush fell over the crowd.

Philippe expertly maneuvered his horse to the side of the street just clear of the watchers, faced in the direction of the approaching tumbril, and waited silently, his hand under his cloak closing around the hilt of a knife.

The tumbril rattled toward him. Stede was standing, his wrists tied behind his back, his eyes searching the hostile faces of the crowd who yelled obscenities and shook their fists.

Behind the tumbril, the road was clear. Philippe dug his knees into the flanks of his horse. There was a flash of hooves, a flying cape, and he swooped down on the tumbril.

Stede saw the glint of the knife, felt his bonds break, and heard Philippe shout in English, "Over your head—a rope." Then Philippe went streaking down the road so recently cleared by the tumbril.

Looking up, Stede saw the rope stretched tautly from the upper windows. He had just enough time to grasp it as the tumbril passed under it. Although physically weakened by the days of illness in prison, raw necessity and the will to live made Stede stronger and more agile than he had ever been. Swinging his body, he went hand over hand toward the nearest window, where a familiar face was waiting.

All was confusion in the street. There were shouts, and the tumbril ground to a halt. Hands reached for him, one closing about his ankle, but he shook it free. A shot was fired, causing screams from the women. The sound of Philippe's horse diminished and was lost in the uproar.

"Hurry up," Chalmers hissed the words through closed teeth, extending an arm to assist his captain. Stede vaulted into the room beside him.

"Come on," Chalmers said, throwing open the door.

They were in the private quarters of the printer who owned the shop below. The printer was an old friend of Philippe's from his pamphlet-writing days.

At the rear of the shop, a closed carriage was waiting. Before the mob had burst into the print shop, Stede and Chalmers were being whisked down the back streets of Paris.

"What about Philippe?" Stede asked, regaining his breath.

"Great horseman," Chalmers grunted. "He'll outride any who chase him."

"And the owner of the shop you used?"

Chalmers showed yellowed teeth in a grin and nodded toward the driver of their carriage. "Meet Gaspard the printer. He's had enough of the butchery. He's going with us."

Gaspard drove the horses down the back streets and alleys and eventually they were rolling along country lanes. Stede extracted information from the taciturn Chalmers slowly, discovering that Philippe had somehow managed to ascertain the precise date and time of Stede's execution. He also learned that there was a waterfront tavern near where the *Tawny Rose* was moored and that Corinne Dubois had decided to stay there to await his return. They had obtained the horse Philippe used from the tavern with the promise that Stede would pay handsomely.

"So we must rendezvous with Philippe there," Stede said, wondering how he was going to explain to Corinne that he intended to return to England to pay court to Darcy Sinclair.

"Another problem," Chalmers said. "Aboard ship."

"Yes?"

"Two more women." Chalmers gave an evil grin. "A Miss Sinclair and a Miss Jones."

Stede felt a rush of elation that diminished a moment later when he realized that Darcy must already have met Corinne.

He glanced sideways at Chalmers, who clearly found his predicament amusing. There would be no point in trying to learn from his uncommunicative first officer what had already transpired between the two women.

Now that they had reached the comparitive safety of the countryside, Gaspard allowed the horses to rest. He was a diminutive, sharp–featured man with bright inquisitive eyes who spoke no English. *"Parlais vous Francaise, m'sieur?"* he asked Stede, and upon receiving an affirmative answer, he indicated that there was a hooded cloak under their seat. "Wear it, m'sieur, when we arrive at the tavern," he instructed. "Your shaved head will otherwise attract the attention of those who do not like to see Madame Guillotine cheated of her prey."

Stede complied, thinking that perhaps Madame Guillotine would have been a less formidable adversary to face than the waiting Corinne.

Chapter Fifteen

THE MOMENT STEDE stepped into the tavern, Corinne flung herself into his arms.

"You are safe! Ah, my love!" She was pressing kisses to his mouth, cheeks, eyes, oblivious to the stares and bawdy comments of the other patrons.

Stede had to keep one hand on the hood of his cloak to keep it from slipping to reveal his shaved head. "Corinne—be careful what you say," he whispered against her ear. "Come, let us sit over there in the corner. I must talk to you."

Turning to Chalmers who stood stone-faced at his side, Stede said, "See if Philippe is here yet—send some wine over to that corner table, then get back to the ship and make ready to sail. Prepare for a long voyage, Mr. Chalmers. Our provisions should be adequate, and get some more water aboard—fresh meat too."

"Done already," Chalmers muttered, giving his captain a reproachful look because he had not expected the *Tawny Rose* to be prepared for the sail to America. "But I'll see about the Frenchie."

Chalmers moved off while Stede picked his way carefully through the crowded room, Corinne glued to his side.

After their wine was delivered, Stede reached across the table and enclosed Corinne's hands with his. "You should have gone ashore in England—gone to the address I gave you in London.

My cousin there would have taken care of you. It is dangerous for you to be in France.''

Her black eyes flashed. "You want to get rid of me.''

"I'm sorry," Stede interrupted quickly. "I let you believe I wanted a permanent liaison—that was unforgivable, but I beg you to try to understand. We shared an *amourette*, Corinne . . . a little love that will always be a precious memory. But I have met a woman I want to marry.''

She froze. "Your tawny rose," she said, her lips barely moving.

"Yes. I never meant to hurt you. When we met, I thought my tawny rose was merely a woman from my Uncle Jean-Paul's past . . . a portrait only, the subject long dead.''

"I should have killed her when she came aboard your ship," Corinne said bitterly. "I would have, but I was too ill.''

Stede said gently, "It wouldn't have changed my feelings.''

Corinne tossed her hair back over her shoulder. She had spent all afternoon coaxing her undisciplined locks into a shining cluster of ringlets. "I suppose you know she is aboard your ship? You have been there first—before coming here?''

"I came directly to the tavern. I have not yet seen her.''

She jerked his hands toward her, pressing them to her breasts. "She can't love you as I love you—she's little more than a schoolgirl. Ah, Stede, you need a woman to love you. Please— don't send me to London. Take me with you to America. You told me that in your country there are no *aristos* and peasants— we can all be equal. It won't matter that I am only a maid—no one will know. Stede, please—''

"Corinne, you're a beautiful, warm woman that any man would be proud to call wife. I can't explain how I feel about Darcy. It is a magical feeling. . . .''

Corinne was silent. She released his hands, stared at him, seeing his soul in his eyes, seeing the hopelessness of loving him.

Out of the corner of his eye, Stede saw Chalmers motioning

that he must speak with him. "Corinne—excuse me, I'll be back in a moment."

She watched him go, his tall, cloaked figure moving gracefully through the rowdy patrons of the tavern. He moved like a dancer with the expert precision of a swordsman, perfectly coordinated.

Corinne strummed her fingers on the table in front of her, her eyes glittering with anger as she squeezed back the tears of frustration. Her volatile nature could accept the fact that love affairs ended, but it was Corinne who ended them, not the man. How dare he?

Her humiliation now turned to thoughts of revenge, and those thoughts helped ease the sharp pain in her heart. She was glad now that Darcy Sinclair's arrival aboard the *Tawny Rose* had necessitated that certain precautions be taken against the possibility that she would usurp Corinne's place with Stede. She smiled a secretive little smile and gave a saucy wink to a man at the next table who was watching her appreciatively.

Stede returned to her table but did not sit down again. "Corinne, you must let me take you back to England before I sail for America. You can stay with my cousin until you choose between all of the rich young Englishmen who will be flocking about you. My cousin is also young, handsome, and quite rich —since I helped him take most of his wealth out of France."

"I am not a piece of goods to be passed on to someone else when you are finished with me," Corinne said coldly. "And I do not want to live in England. I'm told it rains all the time."

"Not true . . . but if you insist on remaining in France, then I will go back to my ship and bring you enough money to live on until you decide what you want to do. I will also give you my address in Philadelphia. You must promise to write to me should you ever need help." He paused, worried about her. "Do you have friends who will take you in? You know you can't go back to the chateau? Where will you go?"

She looked up at him from under a fringe of curling lashes as black as spiders. "I will go back to your ship with you—there are a few of my things still aboard. But you can keep your money. I will not be paid off like some whore."

He hesitated, reading ulterior motives into her guileless stare but not wanting to anger her further.

Corinne rose. "I have a room here. I will go and put on a wrap; it is cold outside. Wait for me." She disappeared through a door to the rear of the tavern before he could stop her.

Stede huddled inside the hooded cloak despite the excessive warmth of the tavern. Several of the other patrons eyed him curiously. Chalmers was waiting near the door, making exaggerated facial expressions that clearly indicated he thought they should be on their way. He had already told Stede that Philippe and Gaspard were safely aboard the ship, the horse returned and paid for.

Keeping his head down, Stede began to inch toward the door, his eye on the rear door through which Corinne had disappeared.

A stout man with a red bulbous nose stepped backward from the bar unexpectedly, a brimming tankard in his hand. Before Stede could detour around the man, his elbow connected with Stede's arm, sending the tankard crashing to the floor.

The man wheeled around, cursing. "You clumsy fool—look what you've done." His fist swung wildly. Stede ducked. Someone behind him shoved him forward into the man's arms. There was drunken laughter and shouts urging the red-nosed man to teach the cloaked stranger a lesson.

For a moment they scuffled, Stede trying merely to move the portly customer out of his way. The man was trying to fasten pudgy fingers about his throat when instead he grabbed the hood of Stede's cloak and yanked it back from his head.

A gasp went around the tavern as Stede's shaved head was revealed.

"He's an *aristo*—he's escaped from the guillotine," someone shouted. "Seize him."

Chalmers moved, unhurried, deliberate, into the fray. The two men nearest Stede found their heads meeting somewhat painfully. A third went down under the impact of a knotted fist. Stede meanwhile removed the remaining obstacles between them and the door by flinging the no longer needed cloak over their heads.

"Cap'n, I think it's time to leave," Chalmers said, in tones soft enough for church.

"Mr. Chalmers," Stede agreed, "You're right."

They raced along the waterfront under darkening skies. A light rain had begun to fall, and the trees were whipped by increasing winds. By the time the small boat Chalmers had hidden amid a cluster of fishing boats had reached the *Tawny Rose*, her anchor was up and the wind was plucking at the crewmen busy unfurling her canvas. She was gliding out of the harbor before their pursuers realized that the man with the shaved head and burly companion were aboard.

For the next few minutes, captain and first officer were busy; not until their course was given the helmsman, sails set and sheets secured, did Stede go below to his cabin to greet Darcy.

She opened the door in response to his knock, her face expressionless.

"Darcy . . . you came—" he began, opening his arms and taking a step toward her, wanting to crush her in an embrace.

Darcy backed away hastily. Gwyneth was seated on his bunk.

"I'm glad to see your head is still attached to your shoulders, Captain Winslow," Darcy said stiffly.

Stede searched her face for a moment, chilled by her reserve and the hurt look in her eyes. "You met Corinne," he said. "She was your grandmother's maid."

"She told me she was . . . how did she put it—your *woman*. Where is she, by the way?"

"She elected to remain in France. Darcy—I'm no angel; there have been other women, but that's all over—"

"Really, captain, it's no concern of mine. Gwyneth and I are here only to ask if we could have passage on your ship to

America. You see, it would be best if we didn't return to England. You did say my grandmother had sent me something of value? So I presume I shall be able to pay for the voyage.''

''The jewels—of course—if your maid will move, I'll get them; they're under the bunk.'' Stede said. Surely the sight of the D'Arcy jewels would help thaw the ice.

Gwyneth stood up as Darcy said, ''Gwyneth is my friend, not my maid.''

''Forgive the error,'' Stede said, feeling the length of the bunk but grasping only shadows. Flinging himself flat on the deck, he peered into the narrow space. It was empty.

Slowly he climbed to his feet. ''Perhaps my first officer removed the portmanteau to a safer place,'' he said. ''Excuse me for a moment.'' But he knew before they ever searched the ship that they would not find the jewels.

Corinne, of course. She must have had them with her all the time at the tavern.

Stede stood on the heaving deck as the winds drove the small vessel down the Channel toward the Atlantic. He watched the receding shoreline and thought of the expression on Corinne's face when he told her of his love for Darcy.

Chapter Sixteen

FOR THE FIRST few days of their voyage, the weather was so rough that captain and crew worked constantly to keep the *Tawny Rose* on course, her canvas intact. As soon as they were out to sea, Stede ordered the crew to reef sail, and he took the helm himself as giant waves battered the tiny ship.

Darcy and Gwyneth huddled together in his cabin, holding on to the bunk for dear life, as everything that was not tied down skittered about the deck. They forgot hunger, thirst, even sleep, as they prayed for deliverance from the storm.

Chalmers appeared with bread and cheese and left a bottle of rum to warm them. His expression and terse inquiry about their welfare left no doubt in their minds that the first officer was not happy about their presence aboard the ship.

They ignored the food in deference to the uneasy state of their stomachs, but on the second day, when icy Atlantic winds penetrated every plank and the damp blankets no longer warmed them, Darcy took a drink of the rum and insisted that Gwyneth do the same.

The fiery liquid made their eyes bulge, and Gwyneth began to cough. Darcy gasped, "Perhaps we'd better eat something."

But the *Tawny Rose* flung her back on the bunk, the rum bottle still in her hand as the ship rolled in the trough of a fearsome swell.

They could hear the wrenching of timbers, the howl of the wind, and the muffled sound of the crew shouting to each other. Shivering, Darcy took another sip of the rum and handed the bottle to Gwyneth.

Suddenly, the great hollow roar of the waves seemed to surround them, and the deck slanted dizzily. There was a crash as a monstrous wave broke over the ship, sending it wallowing helplessly. On deck, Stede was trying to bring his vessel into the wind as his crew frantically pumped water, but below decks the two women were sure they were sinking, and both were remembering the terror of their capsized fishing boat. It had foundered much closer to land than their present position could possibly be.

Darcy gulped some more rum, forgetting to give the bottle to Gwyneth as the ship seemed to have been picked up in the hand of an unseen giant. For an instant, they felt as though they were hanging in space; then the *Tawny Rose* pitched forward, sending them both flying from the bunk.

Miraculously, Darcy fell with the rum bottle clutched to her bosom. As the deck straightened again, she gave the bottle to Gwyneth then took another swig herself. Strangely, it no longer burned her throat.

The ship now seemed to be on a more even keel but was still rolling and pitching. Darcy was surprised to see that the rum bottle was half empty. Gwyneth's eyes were quite bright, she noted, and the movements of her lips didn't make any sense.

After a little while, Gwyneth crawled over to the bunk, climbed into it, and promptly closed her eyes. Worried, Darcy followed, kneeling beside her friend and trying to awaken her. She must have fainted, Darcy thought, slapping Gwyneth's cheek lightly. She did not stir.

A doctor, Darcy thought. I must fetch the ship's doctor. Why have they left us alone so long? Why hasn't someone come to see how we're faring? Indignant, she pulled herself up by holding on to the bunk with one hand.

Might as well have one more drink of the rum, she thought, before braving the world outside the cabin. It definitely warmed one's blood. Taking a step toward the door, the cabin spun in a circle and she sat down on the deck, spilling rum down the front of her dress. There was so little left now that she decided she might as well finish it since she had no idea what had happened to the cork and she certainly didn't want to spill rum all over the cabin and have to sleep with the reek of it.

It took several false starts before she managed to reach the cabin door. This really was too much. There was absolutely no reason why Stede could not have found a sheltered cove to wait out the storm. He was deliberately endangering their lives. She would demand that the doctor see to Gwyneth, and she would order Stede Winslow to head immediately for land. The coast of France could not be that far behind.

There was no one in the narrow passageway outside the cabin. Though unsteady, she was able to walk to the nearest ladder leading up on deck.

The wind sliced into her lungs with the impact of a sword thrust. Ropes had been tied from strategic spots across the dark and sodden deck, and she clutched the lifelines and pulled herself in the direction of the shadowy figure at the helm.

A seaman clad in oilskins, sou'wester jammed low over his brow, did not notice her as another wave broke over the bow of the ship.

Her skirts were soaking wet, and her hair whipped about in the freezing wind, but the fire of indignation burning in her breast propelled her forward without regard for the wrath of the elements. It seemed to her that every misfortune she had suffered had come about since that unlucky moment she stumbled into the path of Captain Stede Winslow, and the time had surely come for her to give him a piece of her mind.

He looked down in surprise when she appeared suddenly in front of him, drenched to the skin, her body clearly outlined under her flimsy dress, her hair a wild cloud about her head. She tottered on the uneven deck and screamed something unintelligible into the wind.

"Mr. Chalmers!" Stede yelled, clutching her as she was flung toward him by the pitching of the deck. "Take the helm!"

The first officer skidded across the deck and grabbed the wheel as Stede wrapped his arms about Darcy. She struggled and tried to kick him but slipped. He picked her up, holding her tightly to his chest as he carried her below.

When the hatch closed over their heads, Darcy screamed, "Put me down. How dare you touch me . . . take your handsh off me, you oaf."

"Handsh?" Stede repeated, sniffing her breath.

"Thash what I said." Darcy blinked, trying to bring him into focus. She felt her feet touch the deck, but he was still holding her very closely, an amused smile plucking at the corners of his mouth.

"I came to tell you," she said, drawing herself to her full height and mustering all of her dignity. "My french is ill."

"Your English isn't too robust either," Stede commented, biting his lip.

"Gwynesh," Darcy said, freezing him with a haughty stare. "I demand that you take this shore to ship at once."

His arm went firmly around her waist and he led her back to the cabin where Gwyneth was snoring softly. Stede tucked a blanket over her.

"Come on, Darcy, she's all right. You can sleep in Mr. Chalmers' bunk tonight; it will be more comfortable than crowding Gwyneth. I don't think either of you are going to want to share the same space when the dawn breaks." His face was contorted now, and his glance had found the empty rum bottle rolling slowly back and forth across the cabin.

Darcy let out a deep sigh, tripped over her feet, and glowered at Stede when he steadied her. "You are—" But she forgot what he was because he was dragging her unceremoniously out of the cabin, along the passageway, and into the first officer's cabin. Pushing her down on the bunk, still with that twisted expression on his face and bitten-together lips, he began to peel off her clothes.

Darcy regarded his actions through the red haze of outrage. "What are you doing?"

"Getting these soaking clothes off you before you catch your death of cold. Be still," he ordered, tugging her skirts and petticoats down over her hips.

She had no recollection of his having unfastened buttons or of his pulling the sleeves from her arms. Her limbs lay limply on the bunk, and she could barely feel them. But when she felt his hands on her chemise she struggled again, batting at him to make him stop.

Behind him the cabin spun lazily in circles. It was quite dark, lit only by one lantern fastened to the bulkhead, wick turned low. Stede's face was caught in sharp shadows, defining the strong chin and high brow. He had very nice lips, she noticed. When she felt him remove her chemise and fumble with her pantelettes she opened her mouth to protest, but before she could think of anything withering enough to say, she was lying on the bunk completely naked and he had turned away.

He fumbled in the chest on the other side of the cabin, returned a moment later with a rough towel, and proceeded to rub her body vigorously from head to toe, overlooking nothing. Then he turned her over and did the same to her back. Finally, he sat on the bunk and, cradling her head on his lap, began to dry her hair.

Darcy could not believe what was happening. A peculiar weakness seemed to have overcome her so that she could only lie helplessly, offering no resistance to these outrages.

"I must go to my french. . . . " she began, trying to sit up.

He placed one hand on either side of her face and looked at her, a strange twinkle in his eyes. "Your friend Gwyneth is asleep."

Then his face was a blur, and his mouth was seeking her lips. "I love you, Darcy," he whispered. "And I do mean to have you. One way or another." He slipped her head to his pillow and she lay back, her heart thudding. As she wrapped her arms around his neck and kissed his mouth, a wondrous feeling blotted out the sounds of the diminishing storm, along with her indignation and outrage.

*   *   *

She lay nestled in his arms, his lips against her brow, his
strong fingers stroking her hair back from her cheek. She felt a
wonderful warm lethargy creep through her body and envelope
her in a warm glow. After a few minutes, she began to drift into
a delicious state of drowsiness. A seaquake, she thought, with a
foolish little giggle, not an earthquake. That was what it felt
like. Perhaps the rocking of the ship. . . .

Stede kissed the top of her head, hoping she would not hate
him in the morning . . . or worse, hate herself.

Chapter Seventeen

DARCY AWAKENED TO bright sunlight, a calm sea, and the most unbelievable headache of her life.

Groaning, she sat up in Chalmers' bunk, clutching her head to keep it from exploding. Her stomach rebelled at the movement, and she retched miserably, losing its meager contents. Mercifully there was a towel lying nearby.

Swinging her legs over the side of the bunk, she saw to her horror that she was completely naked. A searing blush rose upward from her neck and stained her cheeks as she remembered the events of the previous evening.

She felt a wave of shame and, inexplicably, remembered pleasure. What kind of madness had overcome reason? Whatever it was, it had separated her mind's logical conclusion that Stede Winslow was a womanizing rogue from her body's undeniable hunger for him.

There was a tentative knock on the cabin door and she had just enough time to wrap the tumbled blanket around her body before Stede entered, carrying a short plank that served as a tray.

"Coffee. Strong and black," he announced. "And a bowl of porridge. How are you this morning, my love?"

Darcy kicked the disgusting towel under the bunk. "Go away. I don't want anything, and I'm not your love."

"Oh, but you are," he told her firmly, placing his improvised tray on the sea chest. "We have to get married. The minute we arrive in Philadelphia." He watched her with a fond, teasing expression. "You irrevocably compromised me last night, and I must insist that you make an honest man of me by marrying me. I know I can count on you to do the right thing, Darcy. I'm sure you would not have toyed with my affections if you were merely amusing yourself. Therefore, I must conclude that your intentions are honorable and that matrimony is in our future. Of course, even with good weather it will take us five or six weeks to reach America . . . and I'm not sure it is legal for the captain of a ship to marry himself—so we'll have to wait. I just hope you will be able to control your ardor until then."

Darcy blinked in the brightness of the morning, her brain sluggishly trying to make some sense of what he was saying. Her head throbbed, and her tongue seemed to have grown several sizes too large for her mouth.

Stede was placing a steaming cup of coffee in her hand, guiding it to her lips. "Drink some coffee; it will make you feel better."

She took a sip, grimaced, took a little more. Her tongue shrank slightly.

"Can you eat a little porridge?"

She shook her head in alarm.

"All right, just drink the coffee. I'll bring you some warm water and you can wash. I have some clothes for you to wear—one of the younger crewmen is about your size."

"Men's clothes!" Darcy said, finding her voice. "I can't wear men's clothes. It isn't decent."

Stede raised an eyebrow. "It's more decent than going about naked, and your own clothes are soaking wet. Besides, it's a beautiful morning, and I want you to come on deck and see the mighty Atlantic in one of her gentler moods."

An hour later, she had washed in lukewarm seawater with a bar of yellow soap that scratched her skin. The coffeepot had been drained, and she was dressed in a seaman's pullover and twill pantaloons that were too tight in the hips. She dragged the wool pullover down as low as it would go, slipped on her own damp shoes, and went on deck.

The breeze was cool but exhiliarating. She began to feel better with the wind in her face.

Stede appeared beside her at the rail. "I'm not sure those clothes are such a good idea after all," he remarked. "Your charms are likely to distract my crew."

Darcy avoided his eyes, fixing her gaze on the distant horizon. The sky was a glorious blue, dotted with white clouds that sailed like galleons across the sun. Below, the sea was a deeper shade of indigo, sparkling, moving, alive, but always whispering of its leashed might as it slapped against the hull.

Sailors were busy repairing canvas torn during the storm, swabbing the decks, going about their duties with an occasional sly glance at the captain and his lady. The *Tawny Rose* carried only a small crew as she had been intended only for crossing the Channel between England and France. It was a tribute to the skill of all of them that the little schooner had weathered the storm.

"I should go and see Gwyneth," Darcy said, acutely and uncomfortably aware of Stede's nearness. Aboard his ship he seemed even more threateningly masculine than he was ashore.

"I took her some coffee, but she was still asleep. Philippe is waiting patiently by her door. He has also been ill—'though in his case the malady was sheer exhaustion and a touch of seasickness. He rode nonstop from Paris to the sea after a feat that would have daunted lesser men."

Darcy made no comment. She and Gwyneth had coaxed the story of Stede's rescue from Chalmers, who had also been impressed by the frail young Frenchman's courage.

"You're avoiding my eyes," Stede said, turning her face with a finger under her chin.

"I should think you'd be too ashamed to look at me," Darcy said, blushing again. "After what happened last night."

"What happened last night was perfectly natural between a

man and woman who love each other," Stede said. "Don't ever let anyone tell you it isn't. And as soon as we reach Philadelphia we will see a preacher and he will give his blessing for us to make love every night . . . not to mention the days."

"Go away and leave me alone," Darcy said. "I don't want to discuss the matter. It is simply too abhorrent."

Stede's grin faded. "Very well. But I'd like to make something else clear. I am responsible for the loss of the D'Arcy jewels, and I intend to return and find them. As soon as you and Gwyneth and Philippe are safely in Philadelphia."

She turned then, her eyes wide with fear. "No! I don't want you to endanger yourself."

"Why, Miss Sinclair," he said slowly, a watchful look back in his eyes. "Dare I hope that you do care for me?"

"It's just that the jewels are not worth the loss of a man's head. Any man's—even yours," she replied icily.

Chalmers was loping across the deck toward them, moving with the gait of an outsized bear. "Would the cap'n check our course?" he asked without greeting.

Stede said to Darcy, "We'll talk later. When you're fully recovered from . . . your indisposition."

After the two men left her, Darcy stared out to sea, thinking of what Stede had said. Had she been drunk? That dreadful insidious bottle of rum . . . was that what had warped rational judgment? Or had it, she wondered, merely removed the barriers of convention to allow her to enjoy what she had wanted from her very first meeting with Stede?

It became obvious in the days that followed that Philippe and Gwyneth were deeply in love. They spent every waking moment together, strolling around the deck or sitting very close together, their eyes locked and adoring, their hands entwined, their lips occasionally moving to 'speak' to one another.

Philippe quickly learned to lip read and to lip speak and added a new dimension to Gwyneth's knowledge by patiently teaching her to read and write fluently, filling in all the niceties of construction and grammar that Darcy had not had time to accomplish.

Darcy watched and silently envied them. Their love was so pure and true, and there was no third party hovering in the wings, waiting to destroy it. Darcy was sure that Stede intended to return for Corinne, that his talk of marriage was merely a slight attack of morning–after guilt. There was also a deep down uneasiness that Darcy felt in regard to her mother's portrait and the name of Stede's ship, and she did not dare give voice to the true nature of that uneasiness even to herself.

Just before the *Tawny Rose* reached America, Philippe proudly announced that Gwyneth had consented to become his wife and that Stede, in his capacity as captain of the ship, would perform the ceremony. Gaspard, the printer, would be best man.

Flinging her arms around Gwyneth, Darcy hugged her friend and kissed her cheek and mouthed the words, "I'm so happy for you both. But what on earth shall we wear?" The one dress they each had was much the worse for wear and had dried stiff from saltwater. In bad weather when they had to remain in their cabin, they often succumbed to the temptation and comfort of wearing the seamen's clothes Stede had provided.

"It doesn't matter." Gwyneth's lips said. "It is only the confirmation of our love that is important."

Nevertheless, Darcy begged a little fresh water from Stede, and they washed their tattered garments. Gwyneth persuaded the ship's cook to allow her to prepare the wedding supper, explaining to Darcy that she had begun her training at Tregarth Hall in the capacity of cook's helper.

They laughed and busied themselves with preparations and prayed for a fine dry evening for the wedding.

The sun was setting over a placid sea, and Gwyneth was a radiantly lovely bride. Darcy brushed a tear from her eye as she listened to Stede read the marriage service from the Book of Common Prayer.

Philippe had no ring to place on Gwyneth's finger and refused the offer of Stede's ring, complete with Winslow crest, telling him laughingly that he might need it himself shortly. Stede had looked at Darcy, but she had looked away.

Now as Stede said, "Do you, Philippe, take this woman, Gwyneth, to be your lawfully wedded wife, to love, honor and cherish. . . ."

Philippe's eyes shone with love, and his voice was vibrant with emotion when he responded with the words that Gwyneth could not hear but did not need to hear. Darcy felt a lump form in her throat.

Gwyneth had done wonders with the ship's bread, which Stede called "biscuits" although they were anything but sweet; and she had fashioned something closely resembling stew from the dried meat that was all that was left of their provisions after weeks at sea.

There was wine for the toasts and, when the meal ended, Stede said quietly to Darcy, "You can move into Chalmers' cabin—he and I will be busy tonight preparing to land."

Darcy blushed and looked away from his searching gaze. He had been a perfect gentleman all these weeks at sea, but sometimes she would look up and catch him watching her with the eyes of a hungry tiger and she would grow hot all around her collar and in secret places that ladies did not think about.

As Philippe rose and drew Gwyneth's arm through his to lead her to their cabin, Darcy felt a pang of undefinable regret. Darcy stared at her feet, wondering if Gwyneth had any idea of what she would soon experience, and if she, Darcy, should perhaps have explained. But no, that would have entailed confessing that she knew more than she should.

Looking up, Darcy saw that Stede was watching her again, a small smile playing about his lips and a tiny raw flame flickering in his eyes. She stood up hastily, afraid he could read her thoughts, and bade him, Chalmers, Gaspard, and the other crewmen who had shared the wedding feast a good night.

Closing the cabin door behind her, Darcy considered the fact that there was no lock. Eyeing the sea chest, she decided it was too heavy to pull in front of the door. After a few minutes, she undressed, brushed her hair, and rubbed salt on her teeth with a rough piece of cloth. She had been sleeping in her pantelettes and chemise, but the weather was warmer as they neared the American coast and she climbed into Chalmers bunk without then, telling herself this was merely to keep cool.

Chapter Eighteen

DARCY AWAKENED TO the shout of "Land ho! Land!" Scrambling from the bunk, she pulled open the porthole cover and saw a smudge of dark green along the horizon.

Sleep had been elusive, and she felt that she had barely closed her eyes during the long night, but several major decisions had been reached.

It was time, Darcy decided, for her to stand firmly on her own two feet. Her schoolgirl's crush on Cullen Tregarth had been overcome; surely, with time, this wanton longing for that rake Winslow would also die a natural death.

There were sure to be households in the city of Philadelphia in need of a bright young woman to tutor their children. Darcy Sinclair would never be dependent on a man to support her. Men brought heartache and disaster—look at what had happened to her mother because of them.

Gwyneth and Philippe were half way through their breakfast when Darcy joined them. There was a soft, adoring light in Gwyneth's eyes as she watched her new husband while Philippe seemed suddenly older and more self-confident.

"*Bon matin*, Darcy," Philippe exclaimed, giving her a dazzling smile that lit up his light blue eyes. "Is it not a fine day? Let me help you with your chair . . . there. I have just been telling my wife . . . " He lingered over the words, savoring them, repeating, " . . . my wife . . . about Philadelphia. Did you know it is the largest city in North America? William Penn gave the city a theme—brotherly love. I feel it will be prophetic for all of us."

Philippe beamed at everyone around the table, from Gaspard, the bright-eyed little printer, to the implacable Chalmers, who silently consumed great quantities of food. Stede was not present.

"Do you have any idea what you will do there?" Darcy asked.

"Gaspard and I will present ourselves to the newspaper office—or perhaps a printer. We shall soon find employment. Very soon we will go into business for ourselves. Gaspard managed to bring a little gold out of France, and Stede has offered to loan me what he calls a 'stake' to get started. And you, Darcy, when are you going to put my friend Stede out of his misery by telling him when you will marry him?"

"Marry him?" Darcy repeated, raising her eyebrows as if astonished at the suggestion. "Whatever gave you the idea that there was the remotest possibility of marriage between myself and a common smuggler?" Her voice was deliberately amused, and she was scarcely congratulating herself on her acting abilities when Stede's voice spoke behind her.

"If I could have a word with you, Miss Sinclair. In private."

Darcy glanced over her shoulder at him with cool detachment. "When I've finished my coffee, captain."

There was a moment's frosty silence as everyone stared helplessly; then Stede turned and strode angrily away.

Darcy was deliberately slow with breakfast, lingering at the table long after everyone else had departed to watch the approaching shoreline. It was, she thought, easy to maintain a masquerade once it had begun. After a time, one almost came to believe one actually meant it. By the time she made her way to Chalmers' cabin where Stede waited, fuming, she felt she was in complete control of the situation.

"If a common smuggler may inquire," Stede said sarcastically, "What does the aristocratic Miss Sinclair intend to do upon her arrival in my country?"

Darcy shrugged, her glance drifting to the portrait of her mother still hanging in Chalmers' cabin. Looking at the picture was a way of avoiding the sight of the harsh lines of Stede's expression. "I will find a way to support myself. Have no fear on my account."

"You have no money and no clothes," Stede pointed out, his voice becoming as detached as hers. "In such circumstances, there is usually only one way for a woman to support herself. Shall I conduct you to the nearest brothel?"

Her control snapped. Before she could stop herself, blind rage sent her flying at him. She slapped his face and beat on his chest with closed fists. He stood, unmoving, not trying to stop her. When her anger had spent itself, he said, "I deserved that, Darcy. But I had to shock you into realizing that you must let me take care of you and protect you. A woman alone, without means, cannot survive. You know this is so in England—it isn't any different here."

"I can go into service. I'm young, healthy, and educated," Darcy said, sorry she had lost control and striving to regain her composure. She turned away from him and stood under her mother's portrait.

"What is it, Darcy . . . it's more than Corinne, I sense it," Stede said softly. "Tell me why you can't allow yourself to love me, for I know you do. Explain to me why you won't marry me and live happily ever after. We would, you know. I swear to you, Corinne is only a woman from my past."

Darcy wheeled around to face him. "It isn't me you want, admit it. You named your ship *Tawny Rose*—you hung my mother's picture in your cabin where it could watch over you as you slept—tell me, Stede, did you dream of her? Why didn't you put the picture in the saloon of your ship? It's a work of art that everyone could have enjoyed. But you wanted to keep her for yourself. Admit it, damn you. You fell in love with a dead woman—a ghost—and you want me to be her incarnation. Well, I'm not my mother, I'm myself. And I won't play a part for you because one day you'd wake up to the realization that it wasn't your tawny rose you had . . . but me, Darcy Sinclair.'' Darcy tried to stifle the sob in her voice.

Stede gazed at her with stricken eyes, too stunned by her accusation to reply, never dreaming that all these weeks at sea while he had waited patiently for her to accept his love that she was thinking about the portrait.

It was true that his initial attraction to Darcy had been because of her uncanny resemblance to the *Tawny Rose*, but from the moment she so haughtily dismissed the Excise officers on the night of their first meeting, Stede felt differently. He was now certain that the portrait had been placed in his possession by the hand of destiny—it had merely been the device that enabled him to recognize true love when he found it. But how could he explain this to Darcy? And more important, was she ready to believe him?

"I see by your silence that what I've said is correct,'' Darcy said, the mask slipping over her face again. "Fortunately, what you feel for me—lust—is a transient emotion at best. For myself, I feel absolutely nothing toward you. I allowed myself to be seduced like any half-witted servant girl and for that I'm deeply ashamed. I shall never forgive you for taking advantage of me that night. I want nothing more than to have you out of my life forever.''

Stede swallowed, feeling worse than he had ever felt in his life. When he spoke his voice sounded hollow, as though it were echoing back at him from some deep cave. "Will you at least allow me to find you a place to live . . . buy you some clothes? I shall be sailing back to France shortly, so you need have no fear that I will pester you with my unwelcome attentions.''

Darcy was about to give him a supercilious refusal when common sense prevailed. She could hardly seek employment in the tattered remnants of Violet's dress, and food and shelter were a necessity. "Very well," she said indifferently. "On condition that I repay you—in kind—at some future time and am under no obligation to you."

"Done," Stede said, offering his hand.

Darcy took it, wondering why she suddenly felt so let down.

Cullen Tregarth had suffered some particularly heavy losses at the gaming tables. The more he gambled, the more he lost. Eventually, his notes were so numerous and of such large denominations that the other players insisted he leave the game. He had gone back to Tregarth Hall and drunk himself into a stupor.

Everything had gone wrong. Winslow had somehow escaped the guillotine, Evadne and her father had departed for an extended visit to Italy, and Darcy had disappeared without a trace.

Cullen knew he would have to leave Tregarth Hall to evade his creditors. Just as his father had left all those years ago for the same reason. Damn, history was repeating itself with a vengeance.

Coming reluctantly to his senses on the morning after his latest gambling losses, Cullen's body ached with nausea and tension. He did not want to do as his father had done—take a post as steward on some fever-infested plantation in the Indies.

His father had soon gambled his way into part-ownership of a plantation and later, the old comtess had paid Sir Laurence handsomely when he told her he had found her daughter. But instead of returning Regine to her mother, he had insisted on marriage and never told his wife of the reconciliation. The comtess had sent vast sums of money to her daughter in response to forged requests. Sir Laurence used this to buy out his partner in the plantation and to reopen and restore his family estate in Cornwall. Fearing that if Regine ever reconciled with her mother she would leave him, he never told her where the money came from, allowing her to believe that she and her daughter were completely dependent on his largess.

But eventually the old comtess had threatened to cut off her financial support unless Regine was brought to the chateau to visit her. Unfortunately, by that time Regine was dying from yellow fever.

Now word had come from France that the chateau had been overrun by the peasant mobs, the comtess presumed dead. Therefore, even if he found Darcy, there was little chance she would inherit anything.

Cullen had once asked his father why he had kept Darcy's existence a secret from her grandmother. Sir Laurence had replied, "Because, you idiot, there is only one way to deal with women. They must always be kept dependent on us for their very existences. Give them independence and they become unmanageable. Had Darcy been welcomed to the bosom of her maternal grandmother, do you believe for a moment that she would have married a Tregarth in order to salvage our failing fortunes?

"I feel that with luck—and my dear Cullen, I've always been a gambler as you know—Darcy will reach marriageable age while her grandmother is still alive. Once Darcy is Lady Tregarth, anything she inherits is my property. I intend to present her to the comtess for the first time as my wife."

Cullen had understood the wisdom of this. He had accordingly behaved with the utmost respect toward Darcy, solicitous of her welfare, deeply interested in all she did, while all the time flirting with her and conveying the attraction he felt by veiled innuendos and largely imagined stories of his rake's progress. Darcy—and all of her school friends—had been completely bowled over by what seemed to be a wicked but not malevolent enjoyment of life's sensual pleasures.

His valet entered his chambers, bringing water for his ablutions. "Good morning, sir," he said, one fearful eye on his unpredictable master.

"Go away, I'm not ready to get up," Cullen muttered, turning away.

"Sir . . . a young Frenchwoman has arrived. She says she brings you word of Captain Winslow and Miss Sinclair."

Cullen sat up, bloodshot eyes blinking open. "Why the hell didn't you say so before? Get my clothes, man, and be damn quick about it."

Waiting in the drawing room was a dark-haired beauty with voluptuous curves, a sensual smile, and a pair of calculating eyes that Cullen thought fleetingly should be staring at him over the top of a hand of playing cards rather than from under the brim of a fashionably saucy bonnet.

"Cullen Tregarth," he said, bowing slightly. "And I have the honor of meeting . . . ?"

"Corinne Dubois." Her voice was husky, inviting. "And we have met before. Do you not remember?" Accented English, but attractively so, as though she were accustomed to using it frequently.

She was slightly familiar. He knitted his brow. "I am sure I would have remembered someone as charming as mademoiselle—"

"Perhaps," Corinne said, her dark eyes fixed on his, "It would help for you to imagine me wearing a black gown and white apron. A white cap covering my hair. The uniform of a maid, m'sieur, that transforms all women into ugly little penguins."

Cullen's eyes flickered over her expensively cut traveling dress with matching pelisse of a rich burgundy that brought out the color in her cheeks and contrasted prettily with her hair.

"The Chateau D'Arcy—you were the comtess's personal maid," he exclaimed. "You brought me the news that the old lady could not see me—that she was senile and ill. Tell me, what became of her?"

"She's dead," Corinne answered. "Will you please have someone prepare breakfast for me? They offered me overcooked fish at the inn, which I could not eat so soon after the Channel crossing and coach ride.''

"Of course.'' Cullen rang the bell for a servant and ordered breakfast. "My man told me that you brought word of Winslow . . . and Miss Sinclair,'' he prompted.

Corinne smiled a mysterious little smile. "I see that you are eager to hear of them.''

"Winslow is my sworn enemy. He killed my father. Darcy Sinclair is my betrothed. Do you need to know more? I want to find them both.''

"I know where they are. But before I tell you, I have a proposal to make. You see, I also know the whereabouts of the D'Arcy jewels, but I need help to get them. I want half of the jewels—and I can assure you that half will be more than I need to live in luxury for the rest of my life. The other half is yours— along with Winslow and Darcy Sinclair. Since they are hers by inheritance, you can bring them back here, marry her, and live like a perfectly proper gentleman.''

Cullen's eyes gleamed. He took her arm and drew it through his own to lead her to the dining room. "My dear Miss Dubois, I like your practical approach to life. Tell me, did the devil himself send you to me? No matter, I am delighted to agree to your terms.''

"We shall need money for a long voyage,'' Corinne said. "I have used all of my own savings to get to England.''

"I'll get it,'' Cullen promised. "Where are they . . . the jewels?''

Corinne gave a mocking little laugh. "All at once the jewels are more important to you than your intended bride.''

"I am curious,'' Cullen replied, pulling out a chair for her at the dining table himself rather than waiting for a footman to do it. "If you know where the jewels are, why did you not acquire them for yourself? You seem like a clever young woman—I'm wondering how clever.''

"The jewels were in a portmanteau under the bunk I used in

the captain's cabin. Darcy Sinclair came aboard his ship with her maid, and I knew then that Stede Winslow had tricked me into helping him."

"Ah," Cullen said, "and hell hath no fury like a woman scorned."

Corinne frowned. "I do not understand—"

"Never mind. Go on with your story."

"When we reached France, we anchored offshore, and all of the men except for the old cook went ashore. The officer and passenger were going to Paris. The others went for provisions —fresh water and so on. Only the two women were still aboard, but they spent their time either in the other cabin or on deck and avoided me. I was beginning to recover from the *mal de mer*, and so I decided to hide the jewels. I did not want to take them ashore—I did not know where they would be safe with all the revolutionaries roaming the streets. Nor did I know if they would save Stede. So I decided that the jewels would be safer left on the ship, at least until I could think of a better hiding place."

"On Winslow's ship?" Cullen asked.

"The *Tawny Rose*. M'sieur, you have an expression—the comtess used to say it—about not being able to see the woods for the trees? I think that Stede will look for the portmanteau that contains the jewels. So—I take the jewels out of the portmanteau and throw it overboard, weighted down with an iron pot taken from the galley while the cook was sleeping. *Voila*, no portmanteau."

"And the jewels?"

Corinne giggled at her own cleverness and sipped the hot cocoa the footman served her. "Scattered all over the ship, one by one, piece by piece. There are so many hiding places aboard a ship, you would not believe it. There are recesses where ropes and canvas is stored; there are unused kegs and barrels—places where it is easy to hide a brooch or necklace or ring but impossible to store a large portmanteau. The larger items—goblets, and so on. I placed inside the iron pots in the galley. The cook, I noticed, used only one large pot for stew and another frying pan. There were rusted pots stored in the galley in dusty cupboards that had obviously not been used for years. I wrapped the jewels and goblets in bits of rag and worn-out canvas.''

"Very astute of you," Cullen murmured, gesturing for the footman to serve the thick slices of ham and grilled kidneys.

"It took me most of the night," Corinne said. "The next day I went ashore to wait and see who would come back to the ship to sail her away. But that was my mistake. There was a brawl at the tavern, and I couldn't get back on board to collect the jewels."

"And where is the ship, the *Tawny Rose*, now?" Cullen asked, his eyes half closed as he contemplated the sudden change in his fortunes. The French girl was pretty, more intelligent than most servants but sure to succumb to his persuasive powers as easily as every other woman. It would be relatively easy to play her along and eventually secure all of the D'Arcy jewels for himself.

"In America. To be more precise—Philadelphia." Corinne ate the tasty ham as fast as good manners would allow.

"Then we shall have to arrange passage quickly to that distant country, shan't we, my dear?" Cullen gave her a warm smile and passed the platter of ham back to her.

Chapter Nineteen

STEDE TOOK DARCY to the home of his late uncle's physician and friend, Dr. Louis Vedel, who had a wife, widowed daughter, and two young granddaughters in his household.

They lived in a fine old house surrounded by well-cared-for grounds in the heart of the city. The front room was used as the doctor's surgery, his patients coming twice a day at designated hours.

"Doctor and Madame Vedel—Madame Giraud and her daughters Genevieve and Giselle," Stede introduced Darcy, thinking that she would surely be safe in a house full of women.

Dr. Vedel was staring at Darcy. "But my dear Stede, you did not tell us when you mentioned your friend that she bore such a close resemblance to the portrait your Uncle Jean-Paul left with us for safe-keeping."

"Louis, Darcy is the daughter of the woman in the picture," Stede said, avoiding Darcy's eyes. "Her mother died many years ago. Darcy wishes to find a position, perhaps as a governess. I thought perhaps you could help her."

Madame Vedel's eyes brightened. "But my dear, you are the answer to our prayers!" she cried. "Genevieve and Giselle are quite desperately in need of a governess. Why, Stede, you rogue, you knew that all the time."

The two little girls surveyed Darcy solemnly while their mother blinked and appeared oblivious of their presence.

"Will you give us a try, Miss Darcy?" the doctor asked. Darcy said she would, and Stede departed, leaving her newly purchased luggage in the hall for the Vedel's black butler to take to her room next to the nursery.

The *Tawny Rose* was in sore need of repairs, the underside of her hull crusted with barnacles and spars damaged, and Stede knew it would take weeks to make the ship ready for the long voyage back to France. As he strolled the streets of the capital city, he decided it was time to put down roots and buy a house. What better time than now? Darcy was safe and perhaps her new–found independence would be the catalyst needed to bring them together.

They were bound to meet . . . the Vedels were part of the lively social scene of Philadelphia, and he knew they had left any class consciousness behind in the old country. Their governess would not eat lonely meals in her room or be excluded from parties that could be enhanced by a young and attractive woman.

Yes, Philadelphia was a good choice for their permanent home. The seat of government, home of the U.S. Mint, with mail service three times a week and a public transportation service to New York. Since President George Washington enjoyed the theatre, the city's earlier attitude that theatres were of questionable moral value was rapidly changing.

While the *Tawny Rose* was having her hull scraped, Stede quietly concluded the purchase of a house not far from the Vedels', staffed it with a nucleus of servants, and called regularly on his friend Louis Vedel to keep abreast of Darcy's progress.

"A remarkably intelligent young woman, Stede," the doctor told him a month after their arrival. "Does wonders with those two imps. And she's been helping me with my patients in the afternoons when the children are napping. Do you know, she is better with Latin than I am? Don't know how we got along without her. But you know that this happy state of affairs cannot last."

"What do you mean?" Stede asked. They were seated in the window alcove, and he could see Darcy and the two little girls playing croquet on the lawn. The summer sun blazed on Darcy's hair in all its red–gold glory, and she moved with such regal grace as she wielded the mallet that Stede could not take his eyes off her.

"Why, some young buck is sure to marry her, of course. I'm surprised that you haven't asked her yourself. I know all these visits of yours haven't been to inquire after *my* health!"

"I have asked her. She turned me down," Stede answered.

The doctor looked puzzled. "But—she looks at you in that same way you look at her. I don't understand—"

"Don't try," Stede advised. "It's far too complicated. I wonder if you could spare her for an hour or two. Our friends Philippe and Gwyneth have found a house and are moving in today."

"And you have a brand new buggy and sleek horse just begging to take a pretty miss for a ride," the doctor added with an indulgent smile. "Of course. The girls will be taking their naps soon."

Darcy had maintained an air of polite reserve with Stede in the presence of the Vedels, but the moment Stede's carriage pulled away from the doctor's house she said, "I could hardly resist an invitation to visit Gwyneth, but please don't interpret this as a gesture of friendship toward yourself."

"It's too fair a day to argue with you, Darcy. I told you once I meant to have you, and I do. But before you snap my head off, let me ask you if you read Philippe's articles about Citizen Genet?"

The journey passed swiftly with a lively discussion of Philippe's articles about the first foreigner ever granted political asylum in the United States. Genet was organizing anti–British and anti–Spanish movements in his host country, and there were those who demanded he be sent back to France. Since his party there had fallen from political power, return meant the guillotine. Philippe had been scrupulously fair in presenting both sides of the question.

Just before they reached their destination, Stede changed the subject so deftly that Darcy heard him out in sheer surprise. "I've given much thought to what you said about your mother's portrait. It's true I've been haunted by it from the moment I first saw it, but I believe my obsession with it was some mysterious force that wanted me to find you. I'm not saying I believe in ghosts, but some things can't be explained in terms of mortal understanding. You must have felt it—the intuition that warns you to beware. The feeling that you have met someone before, yet you are meeting for the first time. The sensation of having done something before . . . Darcy, some loves are ordained in heaven, I'm sure of it—otherwise, why do two people meet? What strange power placed you at the Inn of the Blue Lantern at precisely the moment I would be there? Destiny, Darcy—ours."

They had reached their destination, and Philippe and Gwyneth came out to greet them. The excitement of the moment cut off any response Darcy might have made.

Between a loan from Stede and the steady profits from Philippe's writing, the newlyweds had managed to purchase a small house on the outskirts of town. Though far from luxurious, it was attractive and comfortable, and Gwyneth often expressed during their visit how wonderful it felt to have a home of her own. Up until the time she escaped with Darcy from Tregarth Hall, the lovely girl had never imagined that she would be able to transcend her servant status.

On the first part of the trip back to the Vedel's house, Darcy and Stede chatted comfortably. The conversation was a blend of lively gossip, spirited argument, and gentle teasing. Then she turned to him, her expression serious.

"I've been thinking about what you said earlier," Darcy said, choosing her words carefully. "I believe I understand why you kept my mother's portrait with you. We are all touched by a tragic love affair—perhaps especially you and I, for we are the children of loves that had to be second best in the scheme of things. And I also feel that you are earnest in your belief that we are destined to be together. That is where the problem lies,

Stede, for although I am not certain that such a force exists, I can understand its allure. You do not love me—how could you? We have had so little time together. You love the very idea of destiny, which is embodied in the portrait of my mother.'' She looked up at him, her gaze clear and honest. "I cannot accept your love right now because you do not see me as a person, complete with character flaws and her own emotions, so please do not press yourself on me in that way. But I do care for you and would like to spend time with you as a friend. Do you think we can do that, Stede? Do you think we can give ourselves the chance to get to know each other?''

Stede was hard put not to stop the carriage in the middle of the street and hold her in his arms. He knew that Darcy had been taught to control her instincts, to be a correct and proper lady for most of her life, first at the Grafton School and then at Tregarth Hall. Now he realized that he was asking a great deal of her. It could not be easy simply to forget all she had learned and follow her heart blindly in a moment. Darcy needed time, and although it would be difficult, he was willing to give her that.

After he had delivered Darcy back to her employers' house, Stede prowled the empty rooms of his own house restlessly, impatient to begin his courtship in earnest. After a time, he decided to go and see how his ship was faring. He had instructed his crew to begin mending canvas now that the hull had been scraped and the carpenters had finished the major repairs.

Stede planned, as soon as he had found Corinne and the D'Arcy jewels, to make a gift of the *Tawny Rose* to his first officer, Chalmers. He and the crew were all eager to return to England and the profits to be made from smuggling, a natural state of affairs since Stede had recruited life-long smugglers who considered theirs a perfectly justified and almost honorable profession.

The *Tawny Rose* sparkled under a fresh coat of varnish, but her decks were strangely deserted. Stede strolled down to the galley, hoping the cook was preparing an evening meal for the crew, who had been living aboard the ship. Perhaps they were all ashore.

In the galley, an astonishing sight met Stede's eyes. The cook had evidently decided to clean out his cupboards, for rusted pots and pans, their lids removed, stood about the deck. On the scrubbed wooden table stood a gleaming array of gold and silver goblets encrusted with jewels. Part of the D'Arcy collection, Stede was sure. He picked up a goblet, fingering the polished surface thoughtfully. If the cook had found the goblets when he cleaned out the cupboards—then where was the rest of the jewelry?

He found the cook slumped at the foot of the ladder leading below decks. Stede slid down to him and turned him over. His skin burned with fever, and he groaned as Stede shook him. There was no tell-tale smell of liquor. Stede threw the man over his shoulder and took him to his hammock.

"Are you ill—what is wrong?" Stede batted away a mosquito that landed on the cook's face. He brought water and tried to press it to the man's lips, but it was spilled as he clutched at his head. "Bad headache, cap'n . . . back hurts, too. Must have passed out. Feel like I'm on fire . . . Mr. Chalmers—"

Stede gave the cook water and then ran to Chalmers' cabin. He too was prostrate on his bunk, his ruddy face pallid. He also complained of a fearful headache, pains in his back and neck, and a burning fever. As twilight fell, the cabin began to fill with mosquitoes, and Stede swatted them to spare Chalmers further discomfort.

"Chalmers, listen to me—it's Saturday evening. I don't want to disturb my friend the doctor tonight. Not unless you think it's necessary. How bad do you feel? Shall I fetch Louis?"

"Be all right till morning, cap'n. Sleep—just need sleep. And water . . . got a terrible thirst."

Stede learned that the rest of the crew had not returned from their Saturday night carousing on the town and that the cook had found the goblets that morning.

"You were both feeling all right this morning?" Stede asked, relieved. Surely they had both eaten or drunk a little too much. What disease came on so rapidly?

Throughout the night the crew drifted back to the ship while Stede tended his first officer and cook, who both had insatiable thirsts.

At one point, Chalmers opened his eyes and said, "Few days ago . . . one of the carpenters went home sick . . . not been back."

Stede pressed more water to Chalmers' lips, thinking that this piece of information was more significant than the fact that both Chalmers and the cook had become ill at the same time.

Just before dawn, Stede went to look at the cook and found blood-streaked vomit beside his hammock. His nose was also bleeding. When Stede had cleaned the clotted blood from the man's face he offered water and was horrified to see that the cook's gums were oozing blood. He moaned deliriously and plucked at his stomach, indicating that the pain was now concentrated there.

Stede made both Chalmers and the cook as comfortable as possible, aroused two other crewmen from drunken sleep to watch over the sick men, then lost no time in setting off for the doctor's house.

As he crossed the quay to the streets, his thoughts finally returned to the goblets. Reconstructing what must have happened, Stede decided that Corinne must have taken the smaller pieces of jewelry ashore with her in France, leaving behind the goblets, which would have been noticed by the person who rowed her to shore in the small boat. Why else would she have disappeared so abruptly on the day of their departure?

He hoped the wealth they alone represented would give Darcy the confidence in herself and the sense of independence that she wished for. He understood this and loved her all the more for her need to be a person in her own right.

Chapter Twenty

THE AUGUST NIGHT passed slowly. Darcy tossed restlessly in the humid heat, drifting occasionally to the surface of wakefulness with a vague feeling of uneasiness.

Twice she got up to go into the adjacent room to check on her two young charges, who appeared to be sleeping peacefully despite the damp warmth of their beds.

In time, Darcy thought, my English blood will adjust to this warmer climate. She went to her washstand, poured water from the pitcher into the bowl, dipped her fingers into it, and patted temples and wrists. Her hair felt heavy and hot and she raised it from the nape of her neck and stood for a moment at her window, hoping to catch a hint of a breeze, but the night was still and silent except for the flitting of insects.

Even the shrill call of crickets down in the garden had stopped, so that when a mosquito whined by her ear the sound was exaggerated by the surrounding silence. Having already collected a score of itchy bites, she slapped at the air, hoping to drive the bloodsucking little horror away.

Returning to her bed, she peeled the sheet back, turned her pillow over, and lay down to think about Stede. For a few moments, her reverie drove away the discomforts and tensions of the long, hot night.

Darcy knew deep in her heart that she loved him, but the powerful need to protect herself kept her from admitting it. She had been harshly taken advantage of by Sir Laurence and Cullen Tregarth, and it was necessary to exercise every possible precaution to keep the experience from being repeated. She could not give Stede—or any man—her trust until she was certain that he loved her completely and unconditionally. In spite of this, a tiny voice within her asked if it were indeed possible that Regine D'Arcy's spirit had somehow guided Stede to her through her portrait. Perhaps too, the yearning of Geoffrey Winslow had touched the *Tawny Rose* and was reaching out to them through an intangible barrier.

She drifted off to sleep, mysteriously troubled by dreams of wraithlike figures that beckoned her to a place she could not see through a haze of dark, swirling clouds.

Sitting bolt upright, perspiration dripping between her breasts, she felt as though she had been snatched back from the brink of some evil pit.

The clamor of voices below her window had awakened her. Dawn was breaking and the sun was not yet up, but already the air was stifling. Going to her window, she was surprised to see a group of people clustered about the front door, demanding loudly that the butler admit them.

Hurriedly, Darcy pulled her nightgown over her head and reached for her undergarments. Patients? So early in the morning? Doctor Vedel's surgery would not open for hours yet. Besides, most of the people harassing the butler did not appear to be particularly ill.

Dressing in her coolest gown, she looked in on the two sleeping little girls and then ran down the stairs.

One of the more agitated visitors had his foot in the door while the butler vainly tried to explain that the doctor was still asleep.

"Wake him up," someone shouted. "We need him."

Darcy went to the butler's side. "What is it? What do they want?"

"They all got sick people at home. They's wanting the doctor to go right over. And him up half the night seeing 'bout the housekeeper," the butler answered indignantly.

"I think you'd better go and wake the doctor," Darcy whispered, taking the door knob from him and opening the door wide. "If you will all come into the waiting room, perhaps I can find out where everyone lives and make some sort of plan of visits so that the doctor doesn't waste his time traveling back and forth over the same streets."

They all trooped into the waiting room, everyone talking at once, all insisting that their husband or wife or child was most in need of the doctor's services.

Darcy sat at the doctor's desk and drew his appointment book toward her. Perspiration dripped from her brow, and she fought a desire to run. Their faces seemed to close in on her, ugly with fear. One man pounded on the desk to get her attention.

"My wife and son are both vomiting . . . black stuff . . . they're in terrible pain," his voice broke, and his fist crashed down on the desk again in a helpless gesture of anguish.

A woman was sobbing hysterically while a child at her skirts covered his face with his hands as though to make the frightening scene go away.

Darcy was scribbling names and addresses as fast as she could dip quill into ink, noting symptoms. "Headache, pain in the back, stomach cramps. Yes . . . nose bleeding? Gums, too? Fever getting higher all the time. Vomiting . . . what? Coffee grounds? Oh, it looks like coffee grounds. I see, yes—her skin has become jaundiced. . . ."

She stopped writing, the quill slipping from shaking fingers. Her lips parted, eyes widened with realization. There was no longer any doubt about what they were all describing, what must be striking in epidemic proportions to have so many cases brought to one doctor. Darcy had read the symptoms many times in medical journals . . . agonizing over her mother's death from the disease.

Doctor Vedel's voice rose over the cacophony. "Please, allow me to get to my desk." He pushed through the crowd to Darcy's side. His tired eyes met Darcy's, and her heart sank at the despair she saw in his gaze. All of these people, herself included, had expected him to appear and, like some all-powerful god, announce that he would quickly heal their sick.

"Darcy, the housekeeper is gravely ill," he whispered. "Go and wake my wife and daughter; tell them they will have to care for the children . . . they are all to stay in their rooms. I'm going to need you to help me." Raising his voice he said, "Now, everyone, calm down and listen to me. . . ."

Darcy sped upstairs to awaken Madame Giraud, who had been only too happy to turn her daughters over to Darcy's care. She was a rather dreamy, lethargic woman who had almost completely withdrawn from life since the death of her husband.

Yellow fever, Darcy thought. *Yellow fever*. How could it strike here? Wasn't it a tropical disease rampant in steamy jungles?

Madame Giraud did not respond to her knock, so Darcy pushed open the bedroom door. She knew the moment she saw the writhing, moaning figure on the bed that the Vedel household had its second victim of the disease.

Racing back downstairs, Darcy collided with Stede, who was crossing the hall toward the doctor's waiting room. He gripped her hand for a moment in wordless greeting. "I came to ask Louis to come and look at two of my men, but I see he already has his hands full."

"Oh, Stede," Darcy whispered. "It's yellow fever. God help us all."

Corinne said, "I do not want to go to Philadelphia. The newspapers say four thousand people have died there of plague."

"Yellow fever," Cullen corrected coldly, regarding her across their New York restaurant table. "And I do not need you to accompany me. I have recruited a band of the toughest waterfront scum I could find, and we shall simply take over Winslow's ship and sail her out of there. You are perfectly welcome to sail back to England from New York."

Corinne's black eyes hardened, "You think I would trust you

to share the jewels with me? You could take Stede's ship anywhere on earth, and I would not know where you were."

"Then come with us, damn it. I've told my skipper that we shall leave tomorrow. His men are impatient for the riches I've promised them."

"But what if we catch the fever," Corinne said, nervously crumbling her bread between her fingers.

Cullen flung his fork down on his plate in exasperation.

"How many times must I tell you that we shall not set foot in that pesthole. We are sailing up the Delaware to Philadelphia. The captain and his cutthroats will tie up alongside the *Tawny Rose*; we swing aboard while her crew is asleep, overpower them, and toss them into the river. The ship and her hidden cargo is ours. By the time the first body floats ashore, we shall be well out to sea. Besides, the reports say that there are bodies lying in the streets. Who will notice that the *Tawny Rose*'s crew haven't died of fever? The plan, my dear Corinne, is foolproof."

"Perhaps Stede has already sailed from Philadelphia?"

"He has not. My captain friend has already ascertained that the *Tawny Rose* was laid up for repairs."

"Then perhaps he has discovered where I hid the jewels?"

"The discovery of the D'Arcy jewels would surely have justified at least a paragraph in the newspaper. Winslow's French friend writes that column that was extensively quoted in the New York papers. He at least would have mentioned such a discovery, if only to balance all the other grim news coming from that stricken city. The *Tawny Rose* is there, and the jewels are there—just waiting for us to go and get them."

Cullen stood up. "Are you coming? I want to rest this afternoon. We have a lot to do in the next few days."

Corinne stood up reluctantly. She had not enjoyed the weeks she had spent in the company of Cullen Tregarth. But without him, the D'Arcy jewels would never be hers and hadn't she earned them after all those years of caring for the old woman?

Besides, she wanted revenge on Stede Winslow and on Darcy Sinclair for stealing him.

"I'm coming," she said. "And I'm coming with you to Philadelphia also. You can tie Stede Winslow up, and I will personally cut out his lying heart."

The fever struck so suddenly that some people did not have time to crawl to their beds. Severe cases of the disease resulted in death within a week of its onset, and morticians were soon working around the clock.

There was little the doctors could do except offer supportive care and advise families to make patients comfortable, destroy their bedding and clothing, and isolate dishes and utensils used by the ill.

The Vedels' housekeeper died the fifth day, and at the end of the first week, the two little girls were orphaned. Then Madame Vedel became ill, quickly followed by the butler and two other servants.

Grey-faced from exhaustion, Doctor Vedel came from his wife's bedside and said to Darcy, "If only we knew how the disease was transmitted . . . we believe it may be by formites, but it seems that even when we burn the clothes and bedding of the victims, their families still contract the fever. And there is nothing we can do to stop the illness from running its course. Are the girls all right?"

Darcy patted his hand reassuringly and poured him a cup of coffee. "I took them breakfast myself. I haven't told them about their mother, I thought it best not to just now. They're tired of being confined to the nursery, that's all. I've given them some schoolwork to keep them occupied."

Since Darcy did not trust a servant to recognize early symptoms of the disease but felt sure she would recognize them in her own body, she had allowed no one but herself to care for the two little girls.

With her English horror of the unfamiliar mosquito, she had also made an effort to keep the pests out of the nursery, as she had been sickened to see fat vectors feeding on the sick. When two more servants died, she was repulsed by the idea of insects going from a corpse to the tender flesh of her young charges.

Doctor Vedel finished his coffee and began to check his valise in preparation for his rounds.

"Doctor . . . you shouldn't go out alone," Darcy said. "Stede told me that there has been a plague of lawlessness as well as sickness in the city. That robbers are plundering the homes of people who have left the city . . . or even those of the dead. He brought me a pistol and told me to keep it handy when you are gone."

Vedel sighed. "I'll be careful. The worst part is not being able to help friends. I went to Stede's ship. Chalmers and the cook are both dead. Three other crewmen are ill, and Stede is caring for them without any help. The rest have fled. You know, Darcy, we doctors say we 'practice' medicine for a very good reason. All we actually do is preside over a patient while his body heals itself . . . or dies."

Chapter Twenty-One

STEDE PULLED A blanket over the face of the last of his crew. The man would no longer choke on his own blood and curse the God who made him.

Walking wearily into the galley to make himself some coffee, Stede saw that the D'Arcy goblets still gleamed with cold aloofness on the cook's table. Apparently, none of the fleeing crew had looked in the galley, and the sick had collapsed too suddenly to become aware of the fortune the late cook had found.

There was no longer any need to remain on the ship to care for his men, Stede thought. He had been desperately concerned for both Darcy's health and her safety in the disease and crime-wracked city.

Since the onset of the epidemic, he had only been able to see her twice, and both times she had been surrounded by people frantically requesting Dr. Vedel's services. He had managed to speak with Darcy privately for a moment and had given her a pistol, praying that she would not have to use it.

The death toll had now reached the thousands, and there was no doubt that the epidemic would be the worst in Philadelphia's history. Among the dead were many grave-diggers, and bodies now lay in their homes with no one to bury them. Even the streets were littered with corpses.

Louis Vedel would no doubt have evacuated his family, but except for Darcy and the two little girls, they had all been swiftly felled by the fever, and those remaining alive were too weak to move.

Stede tossed the goblets back into the galley cupboards, looked at his hands, then scrubbed them with soap and water, trying to wash away the clammy feel of the gold that seemed to bear the imprint of the dead cook's touch. Their beauty and value somehow seemed insignificant in the face of the past week's horrors.

It was too late to visit the Vedel household tonight, he decided; they would all be asleep by now. Returning to his own cabin, he dropped to his bunk. Despite exhaustion, sleep eluded him. He thought about Darcy, wondering if she had escaped the sickness and wishing the night would pass so that he could go to her.

Something nudged the side of the ship. He sat up, listening, every nerve alert.

They were tied to a dock, but the sound had come from the starboard. A vessel on the river must have strayed too close.

Stede got up and reached for a lantern to warn them off. At the top of the stairway leading to the deck he paused and extinguished the lantern. Other sounds, furtive, stealthy, broke the silence of the night. He raised his head slowly.

Shadowy figures were swarming over the side of the ship. Stede ducked and slid quickly down the stairway. Chalmers' cabin was closest. A pistol and the rapier he had acquired in France lay on his sea chest. Stede snatched them up and raced back up to the deck.

A minute later a pistol shot exploded. The boarders dived for cover.

"That was a warning," Stede shouted. "Get off my ship. In three seconds my crew will open fire in earnest. And those of you not killed will be hanged for piracy."

There were muffled comments, grunts, the sound of shifting bodies in the darkness. Then a familiar voice, the slightly bored drawl overlaid with avaricious anticipation. "That's Winslow—I want him for myself."

Stede leapt on deck, charged the nearest man, and toppled him over the side. There was a splash from the water below as

Stede swung up the shrouds to avoid the headlong rush of two men bent on his capture. His boots caught them squarely in their chests, sending them crashing to the deck.

He peered into the darkness, thankful for the moonless night and wondering how long he had before they realized he was the only man aboard. Nor was anyone likely to come to his aid. Ships had been avoiding the plagued city, and those already here were as hard hit by the disease as the *Tawny Rose.*

"Tregarth—call off your running dogs," he shouted. "There's no need for innocent men to die for the sake of our feud. Let it be a fight between you and me."

Seizing a trailing leech, he swung over their heads and landed on the rail above the dock. "I'll meet you on terra firma, Tregarth, your own element."

Dropping to the quay, Stede fervently hoped they would follow. It seemed incredible that Tregarth's need for vengeance had brought him on a trans–Atlantic pursuit. Stede could now see a second vessel, smaller than the *Tawny Rose,* tied alongside his ship. Even in the darkness, it was evident that the raider was little more than a floating wreck.

From the pirate ship came a shrill female cry. "What are you waiting for, Cullen? Kill him, kill him!"

Corinne! Of course . . . the D'Arcy jewels!

A hoarse voice floated out on the river mist. "Ship's deserted, Mr. Tregarth, sir, 'cept for a couple of corpses and her skipper there. You going to take care of him?"

There was a moment's pause, then Stede saw a silhouette appear on the gangplank. "Bring a sword, Tregarth," Stede called to him. "It's too dark for pistols and I don't want holes in the sides of my ship or shredded canvas to repair. Besides, it's fitting that you die by the blade. That's what you intended for me."

From the deck above came a chorus of encouragement and the clatter of steel as someone dropped a sword to the gangplank.

A lantern appeared on the ship's rail, casting yellow light

about the quay. The bodies of three of the *Tawny Rose*'s crew who had died the previous day lay wrapped in canvas awaiting burial. Several coils of rope and discarded shipping crates lay about in disorder. Stede glanced about, noting the obstacles.

Cullen Tregarth removed his coat and rolled up his sleeves with elaborate disdain. The lantern glow caught the blade of his sword and illuminated the sullen hatred etched into his aristocratically handsome features as he walked slowly down the gangplank. "Say your prayers, Winslow, you are about to meet your Maker."

Tregarth was an accomplished swordsman, thrusting and parrying with controlled precision. His fencing masters had taught him the folly of fighting with angry abandon, and he reminded himself to keep the advantage of choreographed attack.

Stede, who was self-taught in the art of swordsmanship, soon found himself on the defensive. Steel clashed, and their breathing grew more rapid. Tregarth deflected Stede's blade and slashed with swift strokes, driving him backward.

"I shall cut you up slowly, Winslow, you misbegotten smuggler. Tonight you pay for my father's death . . . for every insult a Winslow ever hurled at a Tregarth." He punctuated each utterance with savage thrusts.

Stede felt the blade tear through his shirt sleeve and open a long cut down his forearm. Blood dripped between his fingers, making the hilt of his rapier slippery.

Tregarth kept trying to force him back into one of the crates or the canvas-wrapped bodies, and Stede desperately leaped over the shadowy obstacles as he tried to gain the initiative.

The lantern light seemed to be fading. He was vaguely aware of muffled orders, voices somewhere over his head. Then there was the unmistakable sound of canvas flapping free and the turning of the capstan wheel. Damn, they were putting out from the dock. Stede turned his head to look at his ship, and Tregarth lunged, driving his sword for Stede's heart.

Stede flung himself sideways and felt the blade graze his side.

He fell heavily over one of the bodies of his crewmen, his sword slipping from his grasp.

With a cry of triumph, Tregarth leaped astride him, sword raised for the death blow. Stede doubled up, bringing his feet up to Tregarth's chest. He fell forward on to Stede, trying frantically to draw the blade of the sword across Stede's throat.

They grappled in the darkness, forcing the blade back and forth, equally matched in strength and determination, but Stede was beginning to feel weak from loss of blood, and he was distracted by the obvious preparations for sailing aboard his ship.

Rolling over, they collided with the cold bodies of the fever victims, and the tip of the blade ripped into the canvas. A stiff arm flopped from the bundle, falling across Tregarth's face. He screamed as he looked up at the disease-ravaged face of the corpse, inches away, and tried to roll away from the dead man's staring eyes. In his panic, he scrambled away on his knees, clawing at the deck. He pushed himself to his feet, lost his balance, and fell. For a second he seemed to be frozen in the air above Stede, then he pitched forward, impaled on his own sword. Stede whispered, "Thank you," to his dead shipmate.

By the time he had torn a strip of his shirt to staunch the bleeding of his wound and had recovered sufficiently to climb to his feet, his ship was a faint shadow gliding down the river.

He found Chalmers' pistol where he had dropped it on the quay and reloaded it. Tucking the pistol into his belt and placing the rapier at his side, he lay down to sleep.

When he awoke, the stars were fading before the piercing thrust of the rising sun. He uncoiled himself stiffly, remembering that his carriage and horses had been stolen days ago, no doubt by someone desperate to escape the pestilence of the city. He drank some water and then set off on foot for the doctor's house, pistol in his belt, rapier in his hand.

The streets were littered with bodies. His first impression of the grim scene was the silence; then the overpowering stench assailed him. His hand went to cover his mouth and pinch his nostrils closed. Quickening his pace, he detoured around a bloated corpse lying beneath a hovering cloud of flies.

All of the city's business had apparently come to a halt; he could see no one in the shops or buildings. Houses had taken on that forlorn and abandoned appearance that said their owners were either dead or far away.

Several roughly clad men approached from the opposite direction, systematically turning over corpses and going through their pockets. Another band of ruffians was kicking in the door of a house. They carried a sack bulging with looted goods and seemed oblivious of the fact that it was broad daylight. Stede broke into a run.

Chapter Twenty-Two

DOCTOR VEDEL HAD not returned, and Darcy had just put the last able-bodied servant to bed with a cold compress on his head when she felt her own throbbing headache begin.

Fear went through her in a numbing wave, draining her body of all vitality. She clutched the bannister for support as the staircase spiraled dizzily. Turning, she went unsteadily back along the landing to the nursery.

Pressing her forehead to the closed door, she called, "Darlings . . . Genevieve, Giselle, can you hear me?"

There were giggles inside the room. "Miss Darcy, play games with us now?"

"Yes, dear. We're going to play seige . . . you know, like in the story I read to you about the castle. You two are on the battlements and only your grandfather can come and rescue you. Promise me that you'll stay in there and not come out . . . not even if you get hungry. Promise?"

Giselle's voice answered gleefully. "Shall we pour boiling oil on the invaders?"

"Oh, yes. Keep them out at all costs. Don't even let *me* in. Now lock this door and don't open it until you hear your grandfather's voice."

Darcy leaned back against the wall, breathing deeply to try to overcome her faintness; she then moved slowly into her own room. Her bed seemed to be miles away.

She had unbuttoned her gown when she heard a crash from the hall below. There was a splintering of wood followed by gruff male voices; then one of the inner doors slammed.

Intruders . . . in broad daylight. She stumbled toward her chest of drawers and pushed aside her folded petticoats to find the pistol Stede had given her.

By the time she had crept back along the landing to the nursery door, the pain in her head had been joined by a vicious backache, and her breakfast was threatening to return at any second.

Sliding slowly down the nursery door, she sat on the floor, the pistol clutched in both hands. The landing and staircase blacked out then came back.

There were muffled sounds from downstairs. Drawers and cupboard doors banging, furniture scraping across wooden floors. Then the voices again in the hall. Footsteps; the creaking of the stairs as several booted feet began to ascend.

Blinking rapidly to try to bring everything into focus, Darcy held the pistol, praying that the two little girls would not open the nursery door. She had warned them not to let anyone enter for fear that she or one of the servants might stumble into the nursery in their delirium, but now she realized that some sixth sense had also anticipated this new horror.

"Well, lookit," a voice exclaimed. "What we got here?"

She could see four men at the top of the stairs peering at her through the carved ballustrade. Their images were vague, dream-like.

"If you come any closer," Darcy said, "I'll have to shoot." Could that feeble sound be her voice?

There was a burst of laughter. "You been nipping at the bottle, girl, so early in the day? What you sitting on the floor for?"

"You've already found everything of value . . . there are only sick people up here, and if you touch them or their things, you'll get the fever too. Go away and leave us alone," Darcy croaked, raising the pistol a little higher.

She heard more laughter and voices, but the words faded away before she could understand them.

Four silhouettes moved toward her at the same moment that Giselle's voice trilled, "Pour the boiling oil!"

For a second they were faceless shadows looming over her, then the gun went off with a roar that blasted her eardrums and sent her body slamming back against the door.

Stede found Louis Vedel's carriage at the corner of his street, his horses slowly chewing the shrubs that bordered the garden wall of one of the houses. The doctor was slumped over the reins. When Stede touched him, he crashed to the street, his eyes staring unseeingly.

There was no sign of yellow fever on the body. His heart, Stede thought. He had driven himself to heart failure. Bending, he gently closed the doctor's eyes.

The front door to the Vedel house hung crookedly on its hinges. Before he had the chance to enter a shot followed by a man's scream of pain stopped his breath in his throat. As he leapt across the broken crockery on the hall floor, he heard the wail of children's voices followed by scuffling sounds. Racing up the stairs, he tripped over a body lying on the landing. A man with a blood-drenched thigh came to his senses, cursing and groaning. "Shot me . . . hey . . . who are you?"

Stede ignored him in his rush for the landing. By the time he reached it, his pistol was in one hand and his sword in the other. Two men were dragging Darcy's limp body out of the way. There was a bruise on her face, and seeing it, Stede's anger erupted in a molten flood. One man's eyes met Stede's mere seconds before the pistol ball smashed into his chest. A roar of rage came from Stede's lips as he slashed the other with his sword.

A few minutes later, one man was dead and the other unconscious. The third man on the landing was quietly crawling out the door, dragging his leg.

As Stede bent over Darcy, she opened her eyes in alarm and

whispered, "No . . . don't touch me . . . I think I've got the fever."

"What have they done to you, my love?"

"I was sick before they got here, Stede. Please . . . I don't want you to catch it from me. It has to be this way. You see, it was always written in our stars. I believe you now; I believe what you said about destiny. And our destiny is also our fate. This is how your first tawny rose died, and this is how I will die. We can't change our fate, Stede . . . no matter how much we want to. . . ."

She was burning with fever; he could feel the heat radiating from her body. Her eyes were glazed and full of pain.

For an instant, despair threatened to overtake him, but then he wrapped his arms around her and held her close to his chest. "Darcy, listen to me . . . you're not going to die; I won't let you. You're going to get well. You're young and strong and you don't have to die. Fight it, Darcy—don't give in. You aren't the tawny rose—you're my beloved Darcy. Not tied to the past, not doomed to relive yesterday's folly. This is today —now—and it will be *what we make it.*"

Her eyes flickered open again, and she tried to smile at him. Placing her gently on her pillow, he drew a sheet over her body and then went to find water with which to bathe her.

After he had given her water to drink and sponged her burning limbs, he went on a quick tour of the other sickrooms. Madame Vedel must have succumbed at almost the same moment as her husband. One of the maids was also dead. The butler said he thought he was feeling better.

The little girls at first refused to open the nursery door, shouting for him to go away; only their grandfather could come in. Miss Darcy had made them promise. Like in the story about the siege of the castle.

"Giselle, Genevieve, this is your Uncle Stede," he said firmly. "The game is over. Open the door. I need your help. Miss Darcy is ill."

The door opened, and two pairs of round eyes peered around the crack. "Miss Darcy?" they asked together.

"You're going to have to be very grown-up and brave and do exactly as I tell you. I'm going downstairs to repair that front door and you two are going to make lunch for us. We're going to be busy for a while, taking care of a whole lot of sick people."

There was neither night nor day, only a drifting in and out of consciousness and the terror of nightmares, pain, thirst, the convulsive jerking of her body. Soothing hands touched her, water was pressed to her lips, a dear and familiar voice whispered through the agony, urging her to fight, to live.

Sometimes, the dreams took her to faraway places. She was in a coach again, and a gale was shrieking along the Cornish coast. Ahead was the eerie blue light of a lantern swinging slowly back and forth over the inn door. Then the image dissolved, and she was dragging leaden feet through a dreary dungeon, yellow slime dripping down stone walls and hollow laughter all around her as a gaunt face with hooded eyes appeared suddenly in front of her. She screamed, and arms went around her in the darkness, holding her, telling her it was just a dream. But she couldn't be sure which was the dream—was the reality the terror of the dungeon and the dream the loving arms that held her, or was it truly the other way around?

Oblivion then. Peace for a little while, only to be snatched back again to the pain. She didn't want to go back. She was running down a long dark tunnel and that voice was calling her back. But at the end of the tunnel was the sea; she could hear it . . . soothing, lapping, softly enveloping her. She could sink beneath the surface and never have to feel the pain again. But that voice would not let her go.

Then there was only sleep.

Darcy opened her eyes and saw a still figure sitting beside her bed. A sweet face smiled at her, moving her lips silently.

Gwyneth. Darcy smiled back, trying to understand what Gwyneth was saying. After a few minutes, she made out the words. "You've been very ill, but you're past the crisis. Philippe has also been ill but is recovering. I somehow escaped." Gwyneth was pouring water into a glass and bringing it to her.

Darcy's body was strangely not her own. Her brain functioned at a snail's pace, and it was several more minutes before she remembered that it had been Stede who held her and cared for her. Where was he now? Fear came screaming back.

"Stede . . . ? Oh, he isn't ill—he didn't—"

Gwyneth moved swiftly to keep Darcy from getting out of bed. "He's all right. Not sick."

Darcy lay back, her strength spent. "Where is he?"

"So much to do. Burials—the doctor and his wife, the sailors who died on the ship. Sick people to look after. He told me that his ship had been taken by raiders about the same time you became ill. Perhaps he is trying to find out what happened to her. He will be back soon."

While Darcy was pondering this strange news, Genevieve and Giselle peered around her bedroom door.

"Darlings . . . come in," Darcy cried, so glad to see they were pink-cheeked and healthy that she forgot for a moment that they had lost their entire family.

As the two little girls scrambled for hugs and kisses, Gwyneth went down to the kitchen to prepare some food. When Stede returned a little while later, the four were sitting on Darcy's bed scraping their plates. Darcy was gauntly thin, her lovely eyes emphasised by shadows, but it was obvious that her recovery had begun.

Genevieve and Giselle giggled and looked away as Stede gathered Darcy tenderly in his arms. "Thank God," he breathed. "I couldn't have borne it if you'd left me."

Gwyneth ushered the two little girls out of the room.

Later, there was time to talk. Darcy learned that Dr. Vedel

had amended his will when the epidemic felled so many of his household, leaving everything to Darcy in trust for his granddaughters.

"We'll take care of them, of course, won't we Stede?" Darcy asked. She had grown to love the two little girls and, although she did not say so to Stede, had every intention of having several children herself.

His smile lit up the room. "*We*," he repeated softly. "When you use that wonderful 'we' I know we can do anything. Of course, we shall take care of them."

Darcy looked at him for a moment. "Now that I have conquered the fever, I feel as though I have somehow conquered the past." She smiled softly and continued. "Thank you for caring for me, for wanting me to live so very much. You proved that your love is for *me*, and not for a distant, intangible spirit. And even more important, you helped me overcome my own fear that I, like my mother, would die a pathetic death—with hopes shattered and dreams unfulfilled. It may be that we were destined to meet, but I am ready—if you are—to create a life together with no ties to people long gone. I love you, Stede, and want to be with you forever."

Their embrace was tender and filled with promise.

The worst of the epidemic was over, but the last victims of Philadelphia's most devastating outbreak of yellow fever were not discovered for several weeks. Stede brought the news as Darcy and Gwyneth were planning another wedding.

It was a beautiful late autumn day. The two little girls sprawled in front of the fire with their storybooks, Darcy and Gwyneth studied patterns for wedding dresses, and Philippe, also convalescing from the fever, wrestled with the draft of an article examining the various theories of the medical profession on the cause of yellow fever. They all looked up as Stede entered the room. Darcy ran to kiss his cheek.

"Something is wrong," she said at once. "I can see it in your eyes. What is it?"

Stede kissed the top of her head. "It's my ship, Darcy, she's been found."

"From your expression, *mon ami*, this is not good news," Philippe said.

"The *Tawny Rose* was drifting just off the coast. A strange crew . . . and Corinne Dubois . . . were aboard. Darcy, I killed Cullen Tregarth—or at least, he died in a fight with me. He brought the pirates here because Corinne must have told him she hid the D'Arcy jewels aboard my ship."

Darcy's hand flew to her mouth, but before she had time to speak, Stede added, "Everyone on board the ship was dead of yellow fever."

He paused, thinking how vibrantly alive Corinne had been and remembering that Cullen Tregarth had shared part of Darcy's childhood. "The Navy ship that found the *Tawny Rose* sent two men aboard, and they said everyone was dead. There had been reports that some of the thieves who robbed the dead in the streets of Philadelphia had later succumbed to the disease themselves. The two sailors said they had not touched anything, and their skipper decided to set the plague ship afire and sink her . . . with everything aboard."

Darcy stared at him, feeling as he did the ultimate irony of this.

Stede said, "It's all gone, Darcy. Your mother's portrait, part—perhaps all—of the D'Arcy jewels."

Darcy wrapped her arms around him tightly, oblivious to the others in the room. "Stede, perhaps it's for the best. Perhaps it is the end of the past and the beginning of the future."

"All I have ever wanted or needed is here in my arms," Stede whispered, and their love surrounded them as the last of the ghosts were laid to rest.